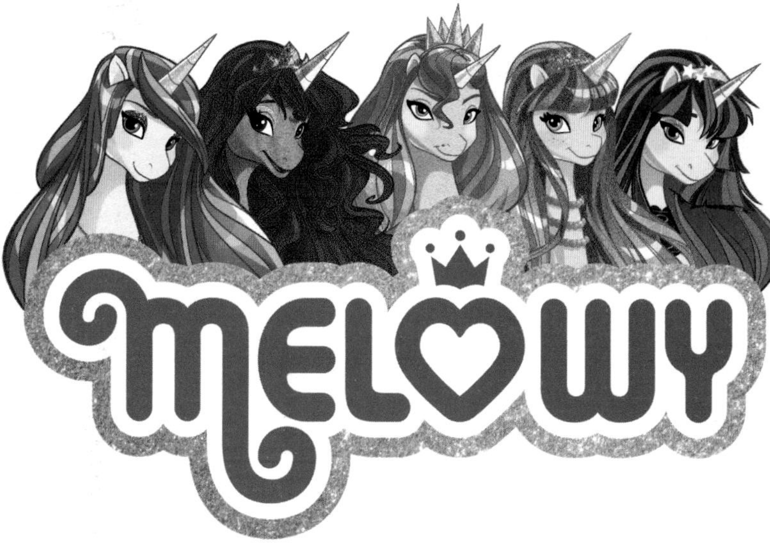
MELOWY

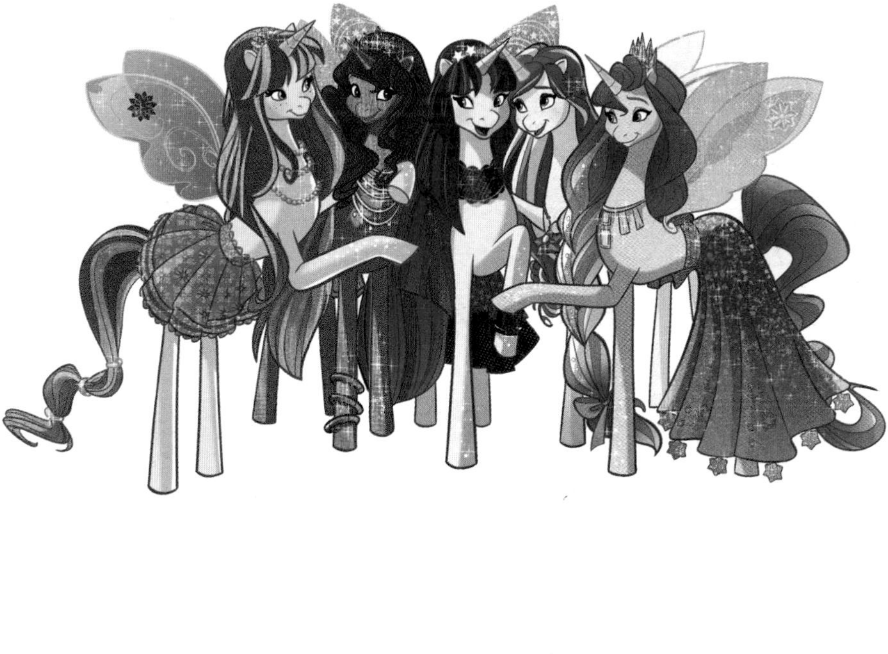

PAPERCUTZ

# MORE GREAT GRAPHIC NOVEL SERIES AVAILABLE FROM PAPERCUTZ

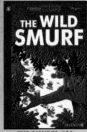

THE SMURFS #21

THE GARFIELD SHOW #6

BARBIE #1

THE SISTERS #1

TROLLS #1

GERONIMO STILTON #17

THEA STILTON #6

SEA CREATURES #1

THE LUNCH WITCH #1

SCARLETT

ANNE OF GREEN BAGELS #1

DRACULA MARRIES FRANKENSTEIN!

THE RED SHOES

THE LITTLE MERMAID

FUZZY BASEBALL

HOTEL TRANSYLVANIA #1

THE LOUD HOUSE #1

MANOSAURS #1

THE ONLY LIVING BOY #5

GUMBY #1

# The Test of Magic

**Cortney Powell** — Writer
**Ryan Jampole** — Artist
**MELOWY** created by **Danielle Star**

PAPERCUT**Z**
New York

MELOWY #1
"The Test of Magic"

Copyright ©2018 by Atlantyca S.p.A., Italia. – via Leopardi 8,
20123 Milano, Italia – foreignrights@atlantyca.it
© 2018 for this Work in English language by Papercutz,
160 Broadway, Suite 700, East Wing, New York, NY 10038
All rights reserved.

Cover by RYAN JAMPOLE
Editorial supervision by ALESSANDRA BERELLO and LISA CAPIOTTO
(Atlantyca S.p.A.)
Script by CORTNEY POWELL
Art by RYAN JAMPOLE
Color by LAURIE E. SMITH
Lettering by WILSON RAMOS JR.

Production – DAWN GUZZO
Assistant Managing Editor – JEFF WHITMAN
JIM SALICRUP
Editor-in-Chief

ISBN 978-1-5458-0003-4

Printed in India
June 2019

Papercutz books may be purchased for business or promotional use.
For information on bulk purchases, please contact Macmillan
Corporate and Premium Sales Department at (800) 221-7945 x5442.

Distributed by Macmillan
First Printing

# THE TEST OF MAGIC

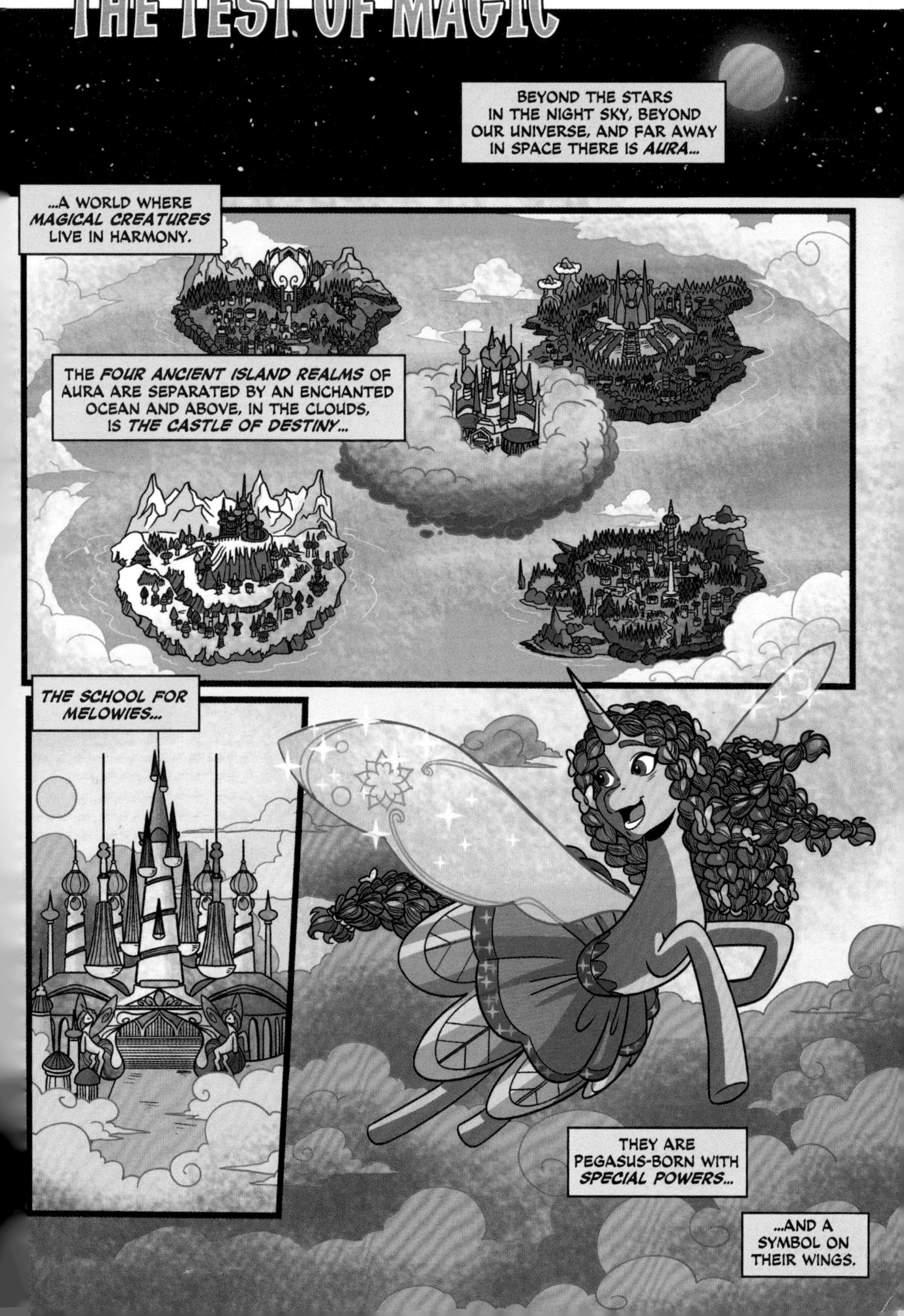
BEYOND THE STARS IN THE NIGHT SKY, BEYOND OUR UNIVERSE, AND FAR AWAY IN SPACE THERE IS *AURA*...
...A WORLD WHERE *MAGICAL CREATURES* LIVE IN HARMONY.
THE *FOUR ANCIENT ISLAND REALMS* OF AURA ARE SEPARATED BY AN ENCHANTED OCEAN AND ABOVE, IN THE CLOUDS, IS *THE CASTLE OF DESTINY*...
*THE SCHOOL FOR MELOWIES...*
THEY ARE PEGASUS-BORN WITH *SPECIAL POWERS*...
...AND A SYMBOL ON THEIR WINGS.

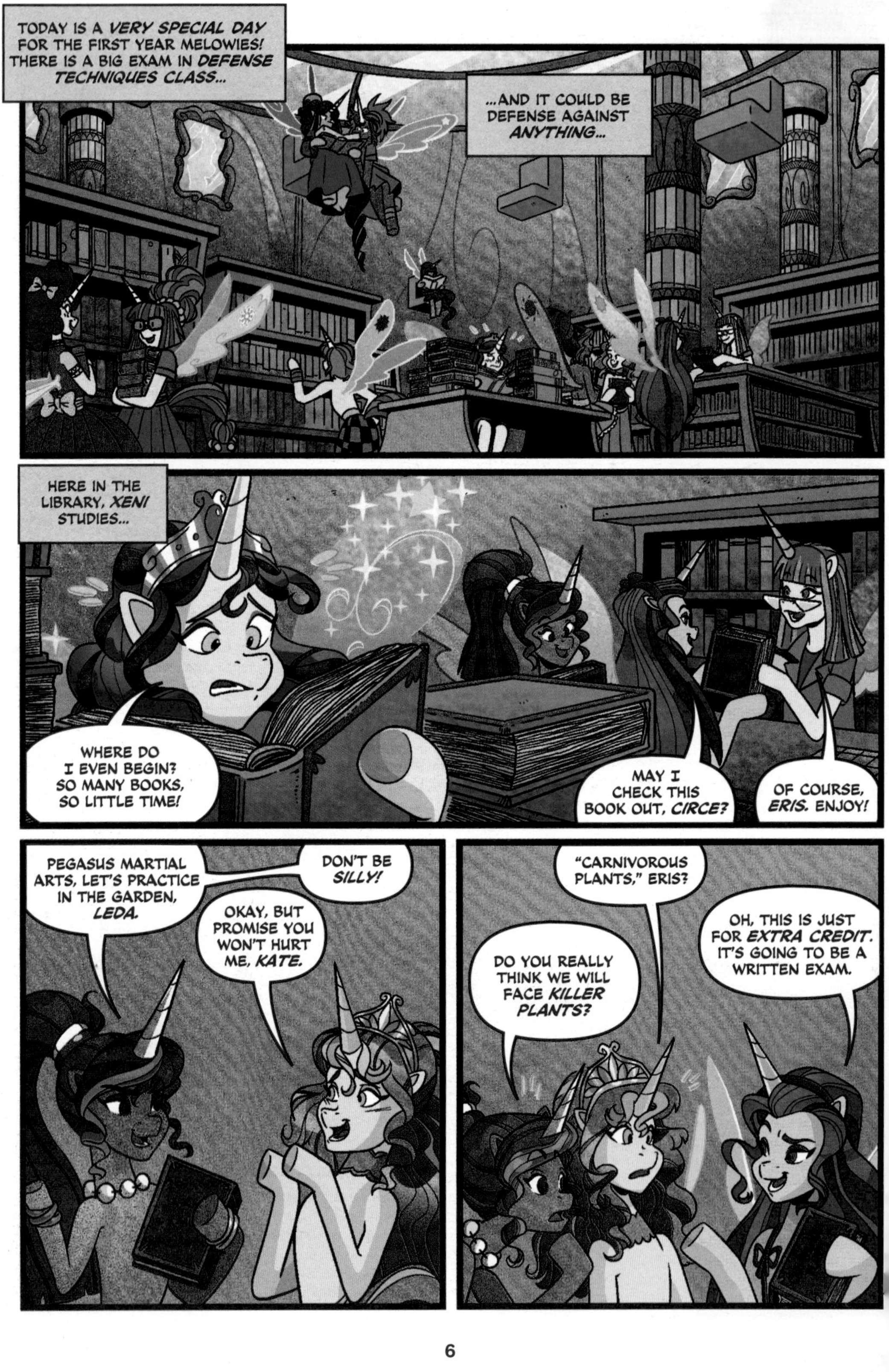
TODAY IS A *VERY SPECIAL DAY* FOR THE FIRST YEAR MELOWIES! THERE IS A BIG EXAM IN *DEFENSE TECHNIQUES CLASS*...
...AND IT COULD BE DEFENSE AGAINST *ANYTHING*...
HERE IN THE LIBRARY, *XENI* STUDIES...
WHERE DO I EVEN BEGIN? SO MANY BOOKS, SO LITTLE TIME!
MAY I CHECK THIS BOOK OUT, *CIRCE*?
OF COURSE, *ERIS*. ENJOY!
PEGASUS MARTIAL ARTS, LET'S PRACTICE IN THE GARDEN, *LEDA*.
DON'T BE *SILLY!*
OKAY, BUT PROMISE YOU WON'T HURT ME, *KATE*.
"CARNIVOROUS PLANTS," ERIS?
DO YOU REALLY THINK WE WILL FACE *KILLER PLANTS*?
OH, THIS IS JUST FOR *EXTRA CREDIT*. IT'S GOING TO BE A WRITTEN EXAM.

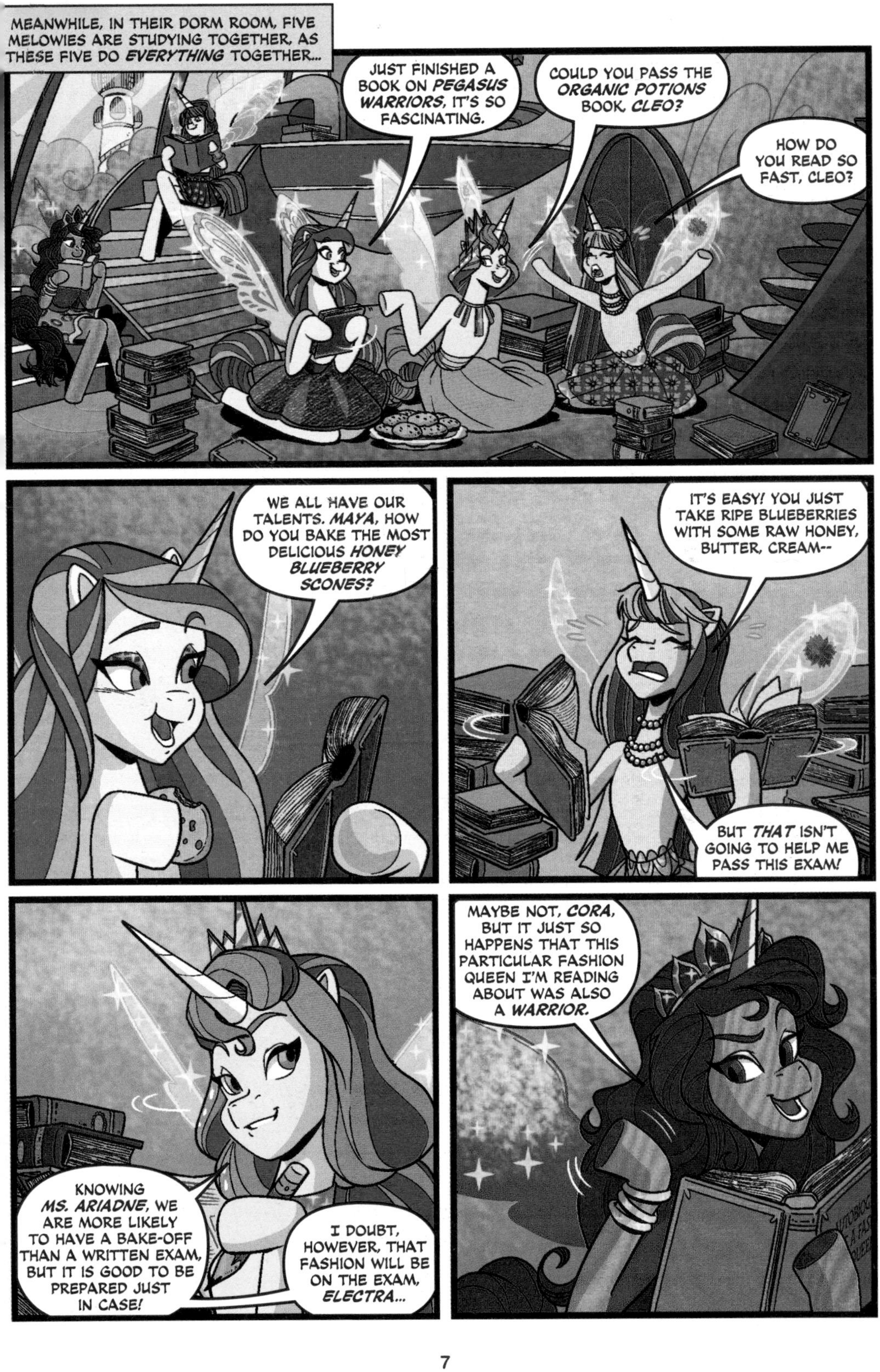
MEANWHILE, IN THEIR DORM ROOM, FIVE MELOWIES ARE STUDYING TOGETHER, AS THESE FIVE DO *EVERYTHING* TOGETHER...
JUST FINISHED A BOOK ON *PEGASUS WARRIORS*, IT'S SO FASCINATING.
COULD YOU PASS THE *ORGANIC POTIONS* BOOK, *CLEO?*
HOW DO YOU READ SO FAST, CLEO?
WE ALL HAVE OUR TALENTS. *MAYA*, HOW DO YOU BAKE THE MOST DELICIOUS *HONEY BLUEBERRY SCONES?*
IT'S EASY! YOU JUST TAKE RIPE BLUEBERRIES WITH SOME RAW HONEY, BUTTER, CREAM--
BUT *THAT* ISN'T GOING TO HELP ME PASS THIS EXAM!
KNOWING *MS. ARIADNE*, WE ARE MORE LIKELY TO HAVE A BAKE-OFF THAN A WRITTEN EXAM, BUT IT IS GOOD TO BE PREPARED JUST IN CASE!
I DOUBT, HOWEVER, THAT FASHION WILL BE ON THE EXAM, *ELECTRA*...
MAYBE NOT, *CORA*, BUT IT JUST SO HAPPENS THAT THIS PARTICULAR FASHION QUEEN I'M READING ABOUT WAS ALSO A *WARRIOR*.

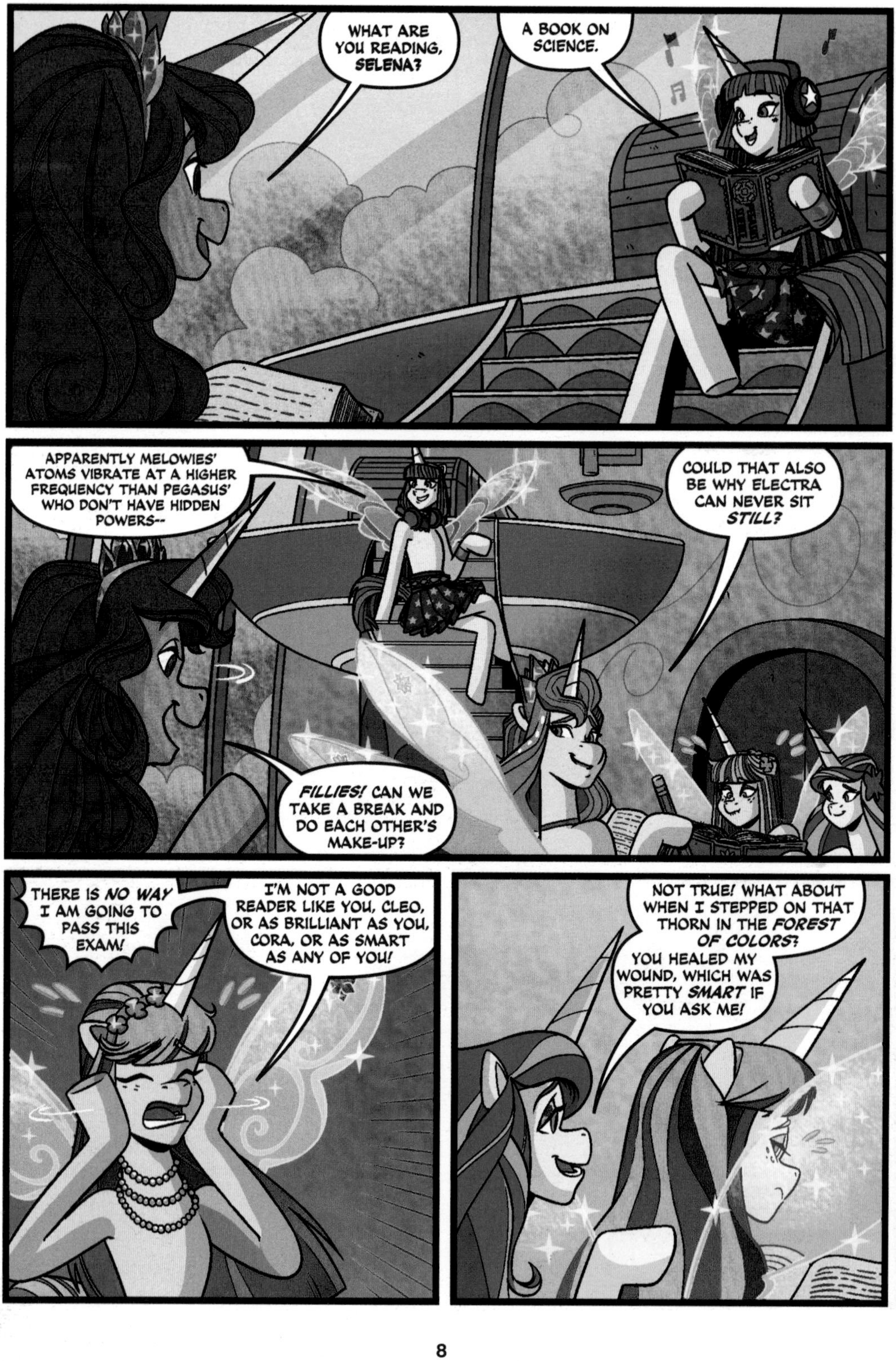

WHAT ARE YOU READING, SELENA?
A BOOK ON SCIENCE.
APPARENTLY MELOWIES' ATOMS VIBRATE AT A HIGHER FREQUENCY THAN PEGASUS' WHO DON'T HAVE HIDDEN POWERS--
COULD THAT ALSO BE WHY ELECTRA CAN NEVER SIT *STILL?*
*FILLIES!* CAN WE TAKE A BREAK AND DO EACH OTHER'S MAKE-UP?
THERE IS *NO WAY* I AM GOING TO PASS THIS EXAM!
I'M NOT A GOOD READER LIKE YOU, CLEO, OR AS BRILLIANT AS YOU, CORA, OR AS SMART AS ANY OF YOU!
NOT TRUE! WHAT ABOUT WHEN I STEPPED ON THAT THORN IN THE *FOREST OF COLORS?*
YOU HEALED MY WOUND, WHICH WAS PRETTY *SMART* IF YOU ASK ME!

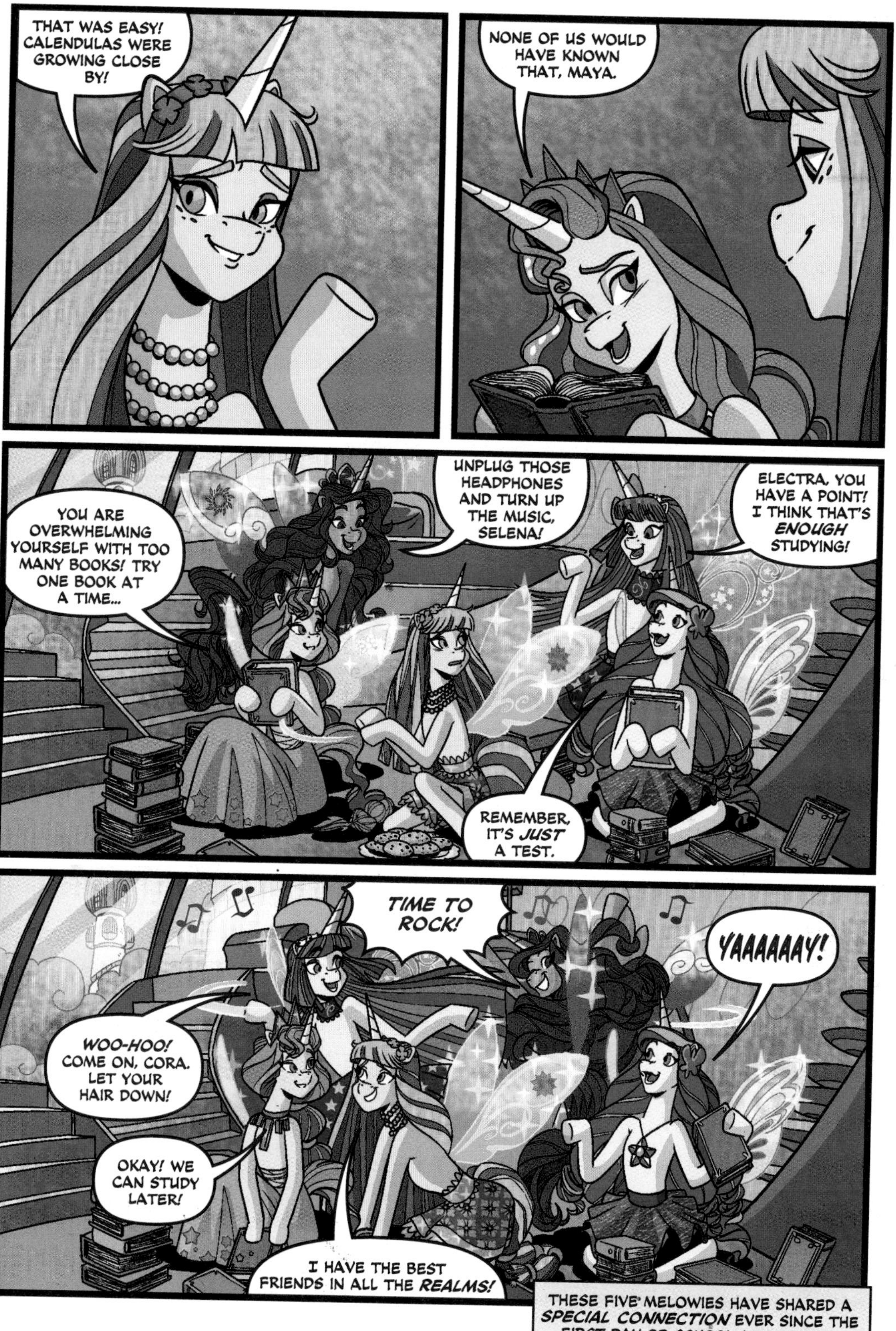
THAT WAS EASY! CALENDULAS WERE GROWING CLOSE BY!
NONE OF US WOULD HAVE KNOWN THAT, MAYA.
YOU ARE OVERWHELMING YOURSELF WITH TOO MANY BOOKS! TRY ONE BOOK AT A TIME...
UNPLUG THOSE HEADPHONES AND TURN UP THE MUSIC, SELENA!
ELECTRA, YOU HAVE A POINT! I THINK THAT'S *ENOUGH* STUDYING!
REMEMBER, IT'S *JUST* A TEST.
*TIME TO ROCK!*
YAAAAAAY!
*WOO-HOO!* COME ON, CORA. LET YOUR HAIR DOWN!
OKAY! WE CAN STUDY LATER!
I HAVE THE BEST FRIENDS IN ALL THE *REALMS!*

THESE FIVE MELOWIES HAVE SHARED A *SPECIAL CONNECTION* EVER SINCE THE FIRST DAY OF SCHOOL AT DESTINY...

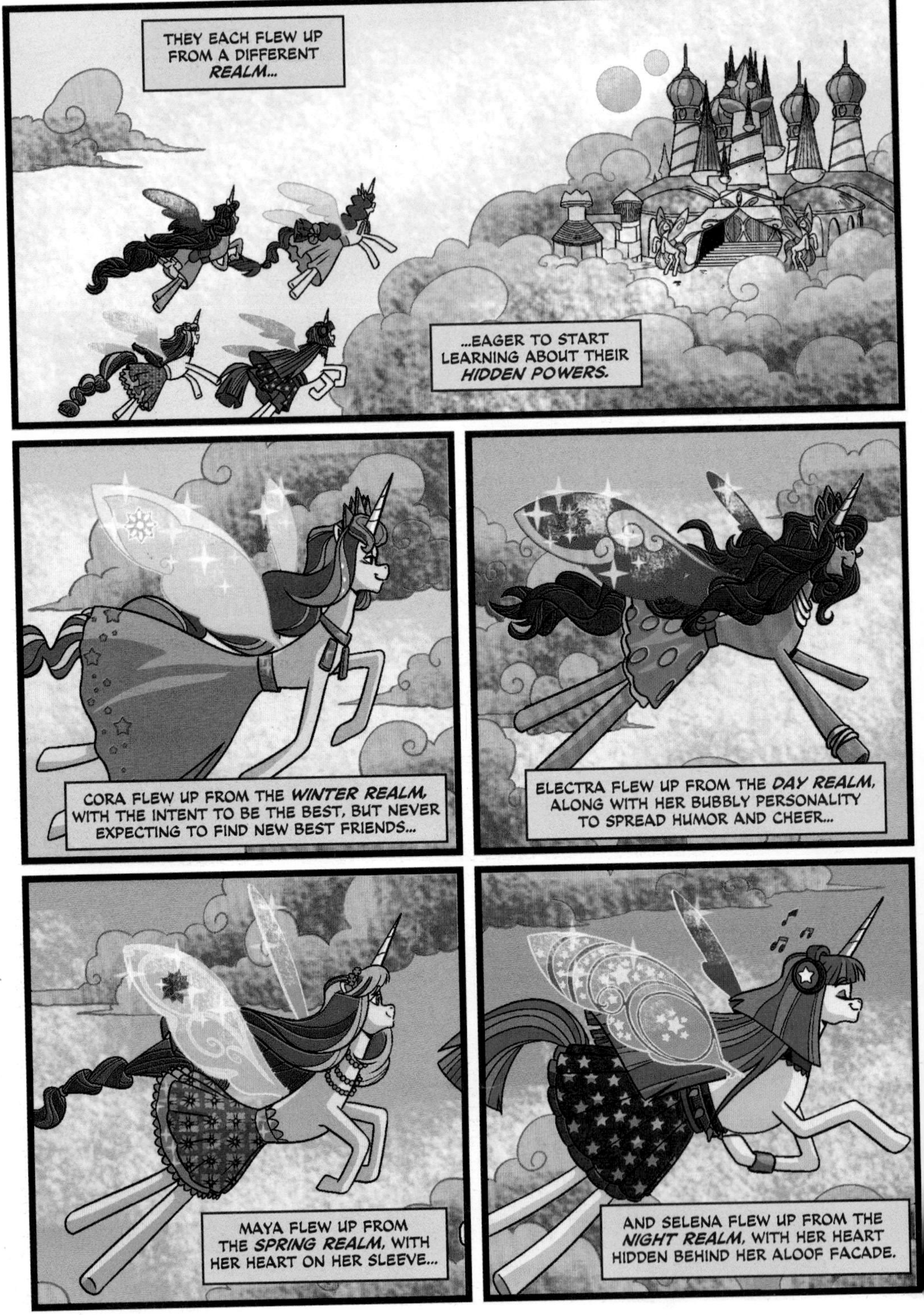
THEY EACH FLEW UP FROM A DIFFERENT *REALM*...
...EAGER TO START LEARNING ABOUT THEIR *HIDDEN POWERS.*
CORA FLEW UP FROM THE *WINTER REALM,* WITH THE INTENT TO BE THE BEST, BUT NEVER EXPECTING TO FIND NEW BEST FRIENDS...
ELECTRA FLEW UP FROM THE *DAY REALM,* ALONG WITH HER BUBBLY PERSONALITY TO SPREAD HUMOR AND CHEER...
MAYA FLEW UP FROM THE *SPRING REALM,* WITH HER HEART ON HER SLEEVE...
AND SELENA FLEW UP FROM THE *NIGHT REALM,* WITH HER HEART HIDDEN BEHIND HER ALOOF FACADE.

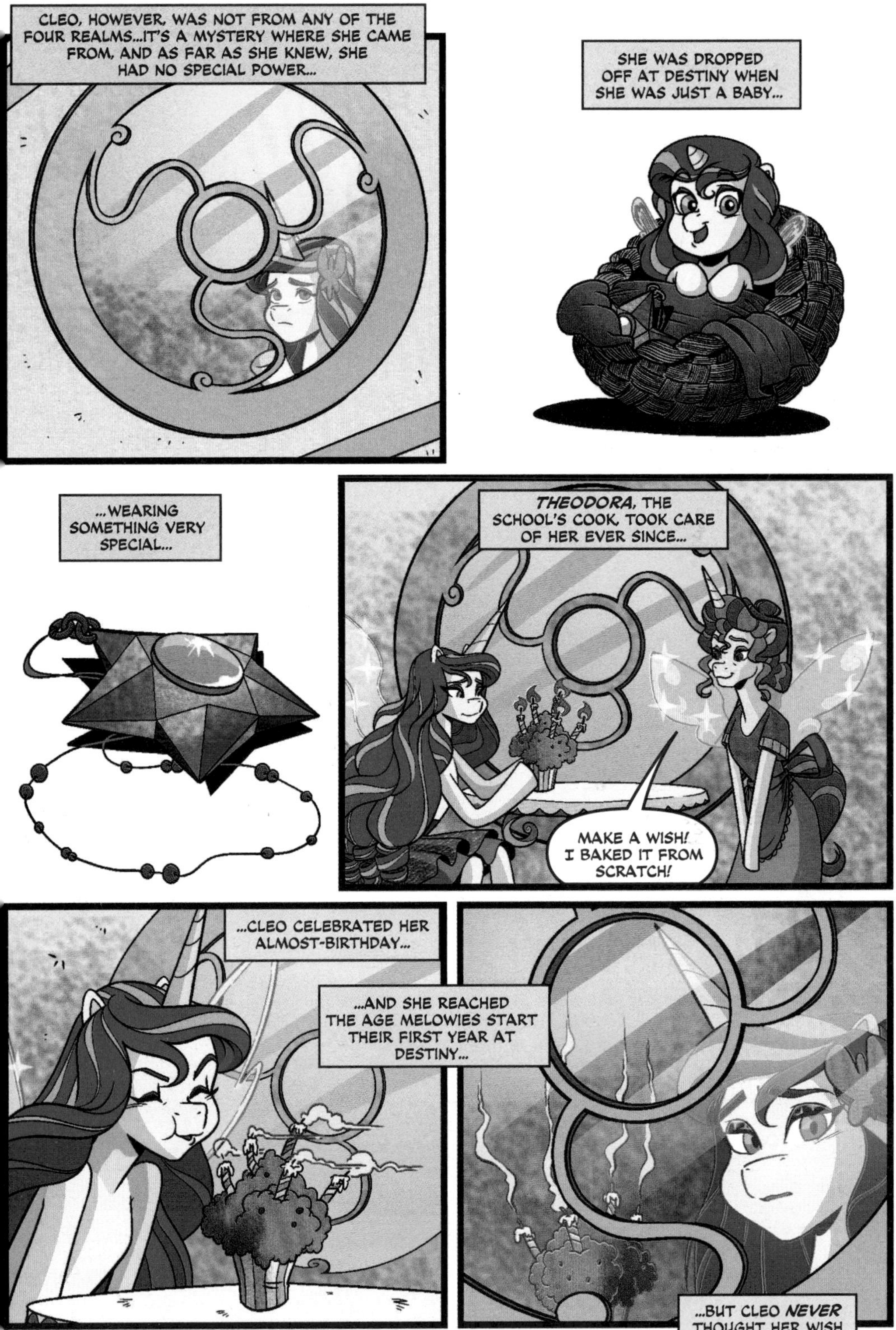
CLEO, HOWEVER, WAS NOT FROM ANY OF THE FOUR REALMS...IT'S A MYSTERY WHERE SHE CAME FROM, AND AS FAR AS SHE KNEW, SHE HAD NO SPECIAL POWER...
SHE WAS DROPPED OFF AT DESTINY WHEN SHE WAS JUST A BABY...
...WEARING SOMETHING VERY SPECIAL...
*THEODORA*, THE SCHOOL'S COOK, TOOK CARE OF HER EVER SINCE...
MAKE A WISH! I BAKED IT FROM SCRATCH!
...CLEO CELEBRATED HER ALMOST-BIRTHDAY...
...AND SHE REACHED THE AGE MELOWIES START THEIR FIRST YEAR AT DESTINY...
...BUT CLEO *NEVER* THOUGHT HER WISH WOULD COME TRUE.

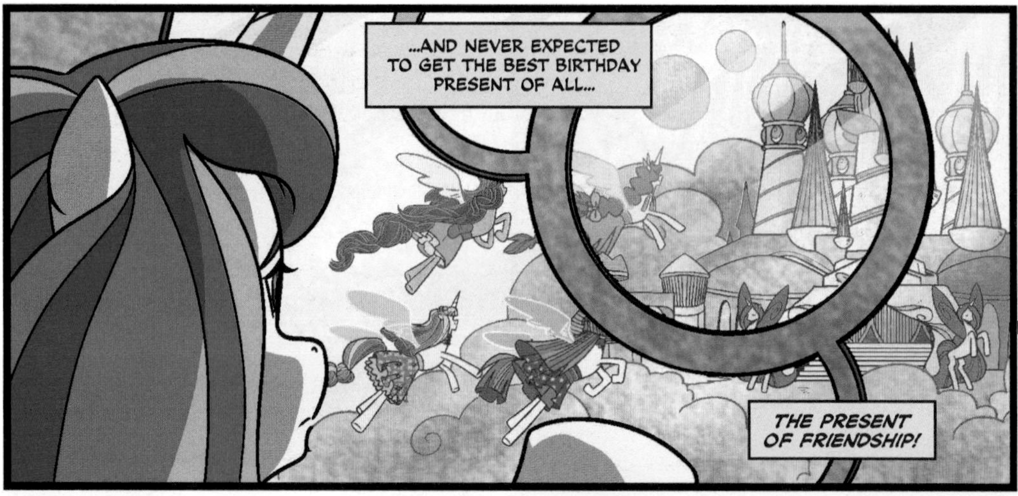
...AND NEVER EXPECTED TO GET THE BEST BIRTHDAY PRESENT OF ALL...
THE PRESENT OF FRIENDSHIP!

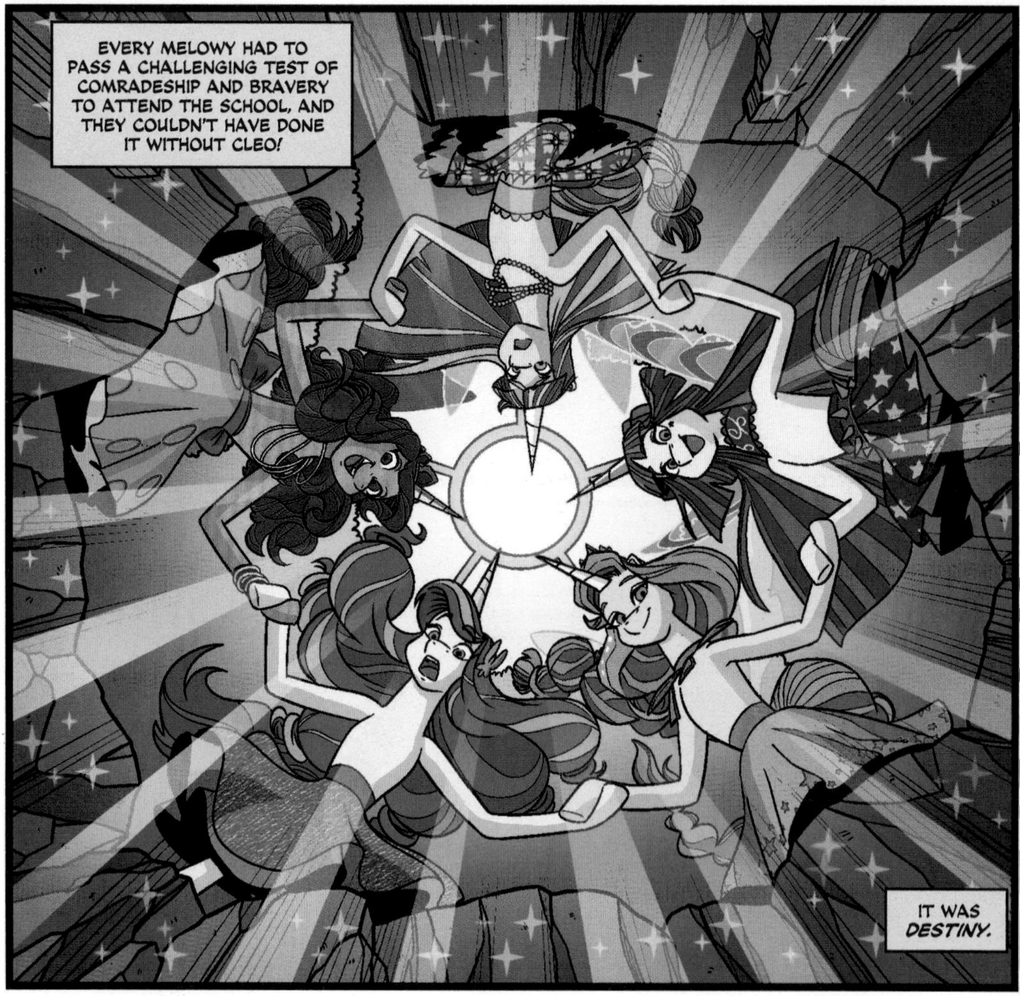
EVERY MELOWY HAD TO PASS A CHALLENGING TEST OF COMRADESHIP AND BRAVERY TO ATTEND THE SCHOOL, AND THEY COULDN'T HAVE DONE IT WITHOUT CLEO!
IT WAS *DESTINY.*

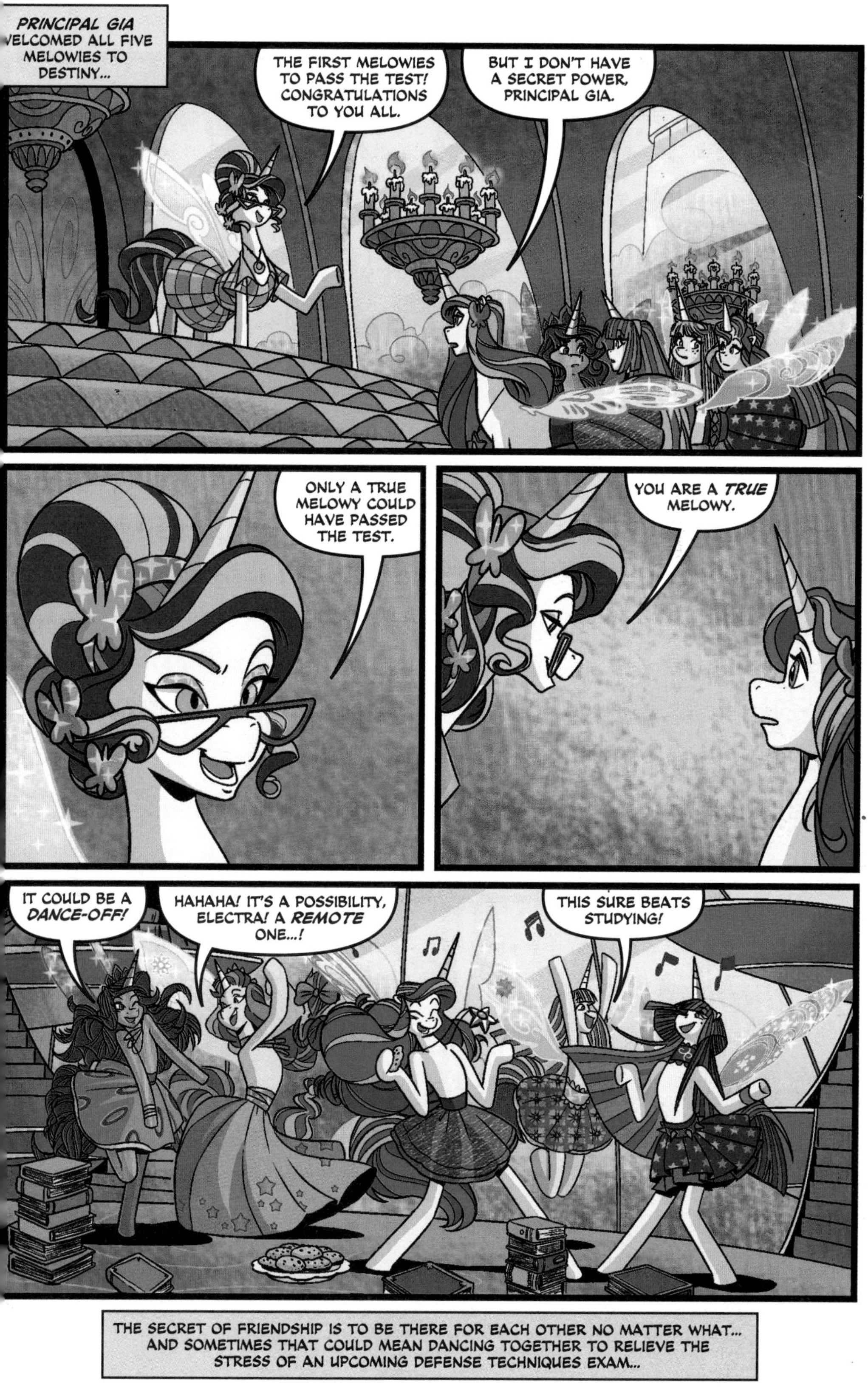
PRINCIPAL GIA WELCOMED ALL FIVE MELOWIES TO DESTINY...
THE FIRST MELOWIES TO PASS THE TEST! CONGRATULATIONS TO YOU ALL.
BUT I DON'T HAVE A SECRET POWER, PRINCIPAL GIA.
ONLY A TRUE MELOWY COULD HAVE PASSED THE TEST.
YOU ARE A *TRUE* MELOWY.
IT COULD BE A *DANCE-OFF!*
HAHAHA! IT'S A POSSIBILITY, ELECTRA! A *REMOTE* ONE...!
THIS SURE BEATS STUDYING!
THE SECRET OF FRIENDSHIP IS TO BE THERE FOR EACH OTHER NO MATTER WHAT... AND SOMETIMES THAT COULD MEAN DANCING TOGETHER TO RELIEVE THE STRESS OF AN UPCOMING DEFENSE TECHNIQUES EXAM...

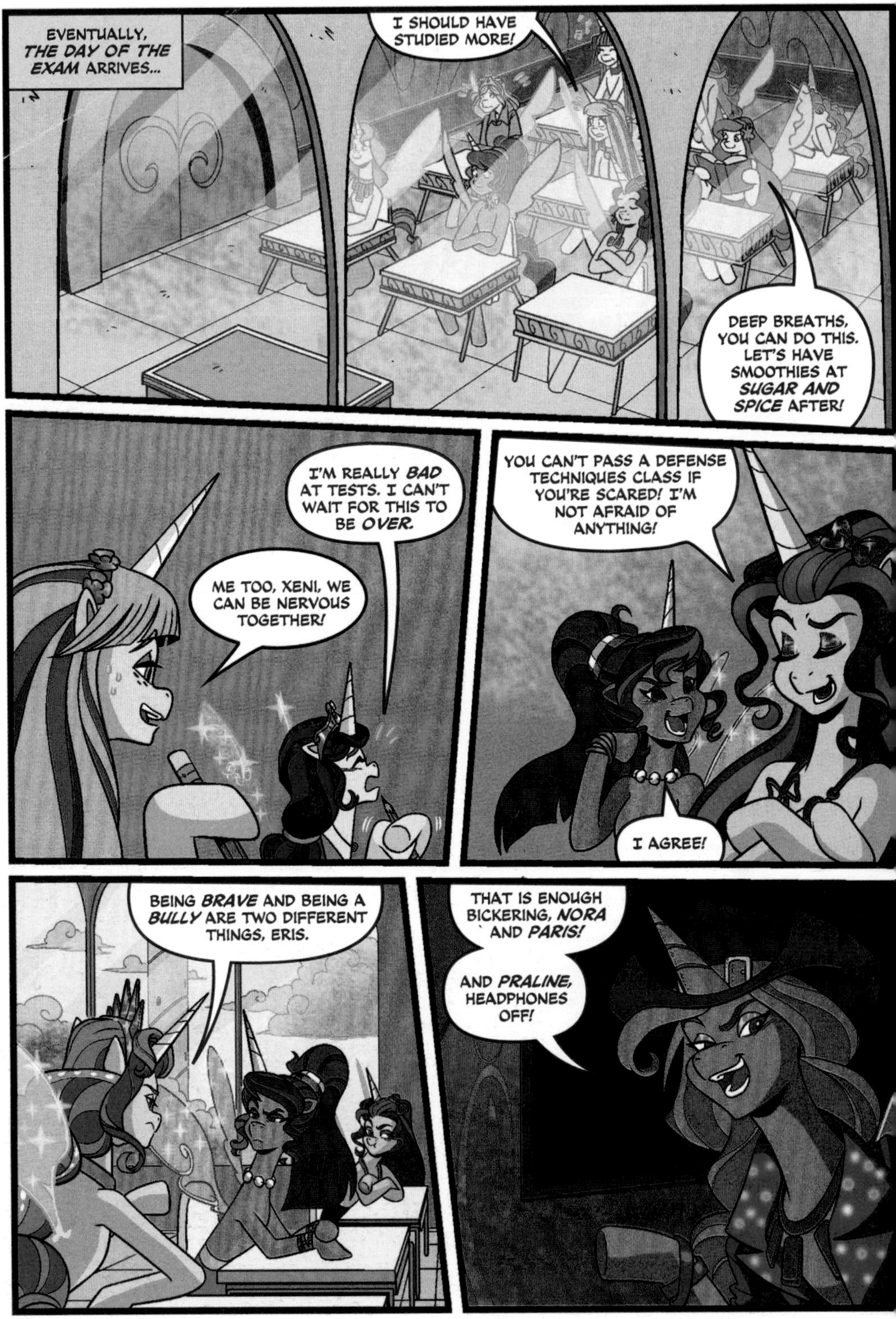

EVENTUALLY, THE DAY OF THE EXAM ARRIVES...
I SHOULD HAVE STUDIED MORE!
DEEP BREATHS, YOU CAN DO THIS. LET'S HAVE SMOOTHIES AT SUGAR AND SPICE AFTER!
I'M REALLY BAD AT TESTS. I CAN'T WAIT FOR THIS TO BE OVER.
ME TOO, XENI, WE CAN BE NERVOUS TOGETHER!
YOU CAN'T PASS A DEFENSE TECHNIQUES CLASS IF YOU'RE SCARED! I'M NOT AFRAID OF ANYTHING!
I AGREE!
BEING BRAVE AND BEING A BULLY ARE TWO DIFFERENT THINGS, ERIS.
THAT IS ENOUGH BICKERING, NORA AND PARIS!
AND PRALINE, HEADPHONES OFF!

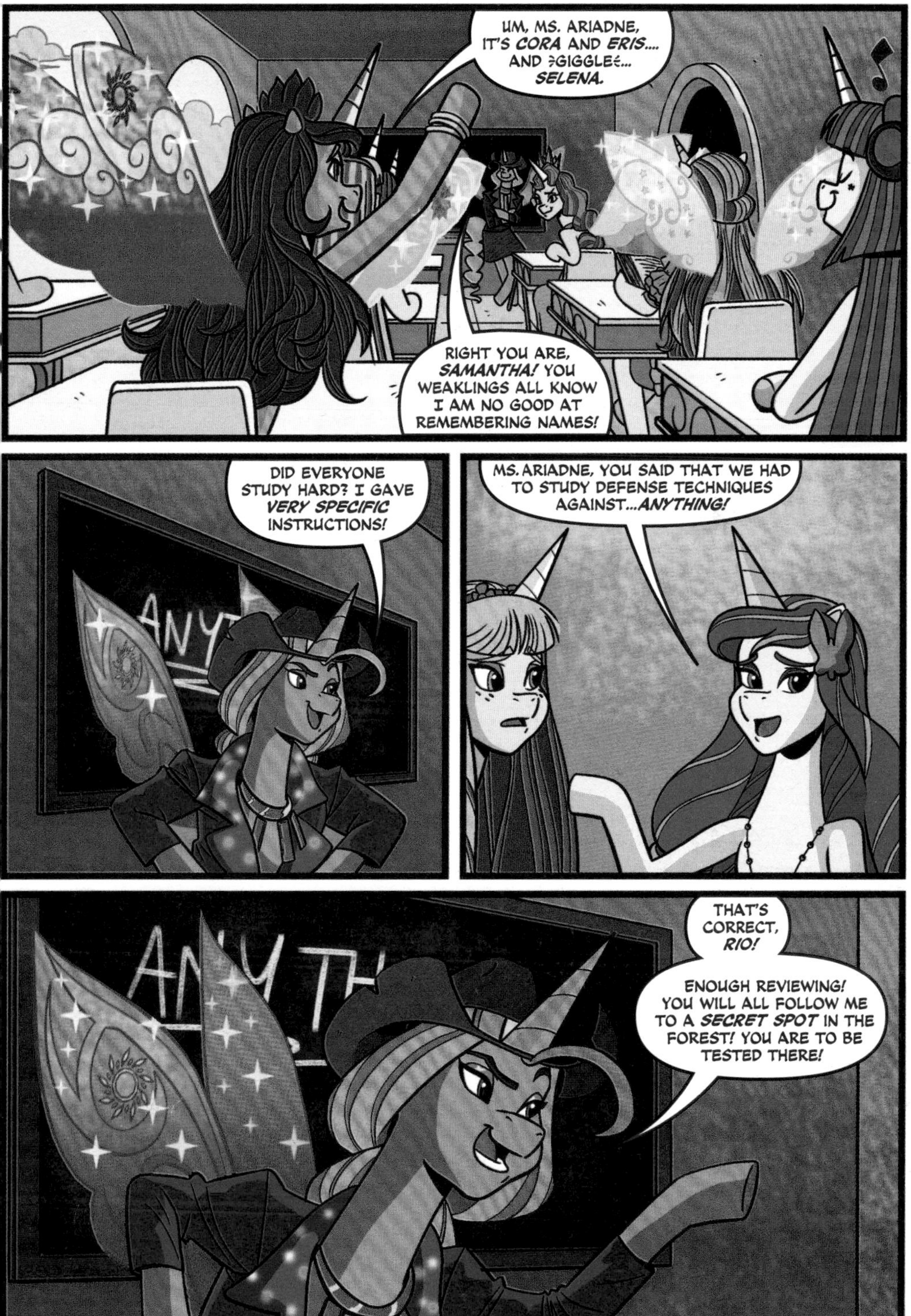
UM, MS. ARIADNE, IT'S CORA AND ERIS.... AND ≥GIGGLE≤... SELENA.
RIGHT YOU ARE, SAMANTHA! YOU WEAKLINGS ALL KNOW I AM NO GOOD AT REMEMBERING NAMES!
DID EVERYONE STUDY HARD? I GAVE VERY SPECIFIC INSTRUCTIONS!
ANY
MS. ARIADNE, YOU SAID THAT WE HAD TO STUDY DEFENSE TECHNIQUES AGAINST...ANYTHING!
ANY TH
THAT'S CORRECT, RIO!
ENOUGH REVIEWING! YOU WILL ALL FOLLOW ME TO A SECRET SPOT IN THE FOREST! YOU ARE TO BE TESTED THERE!

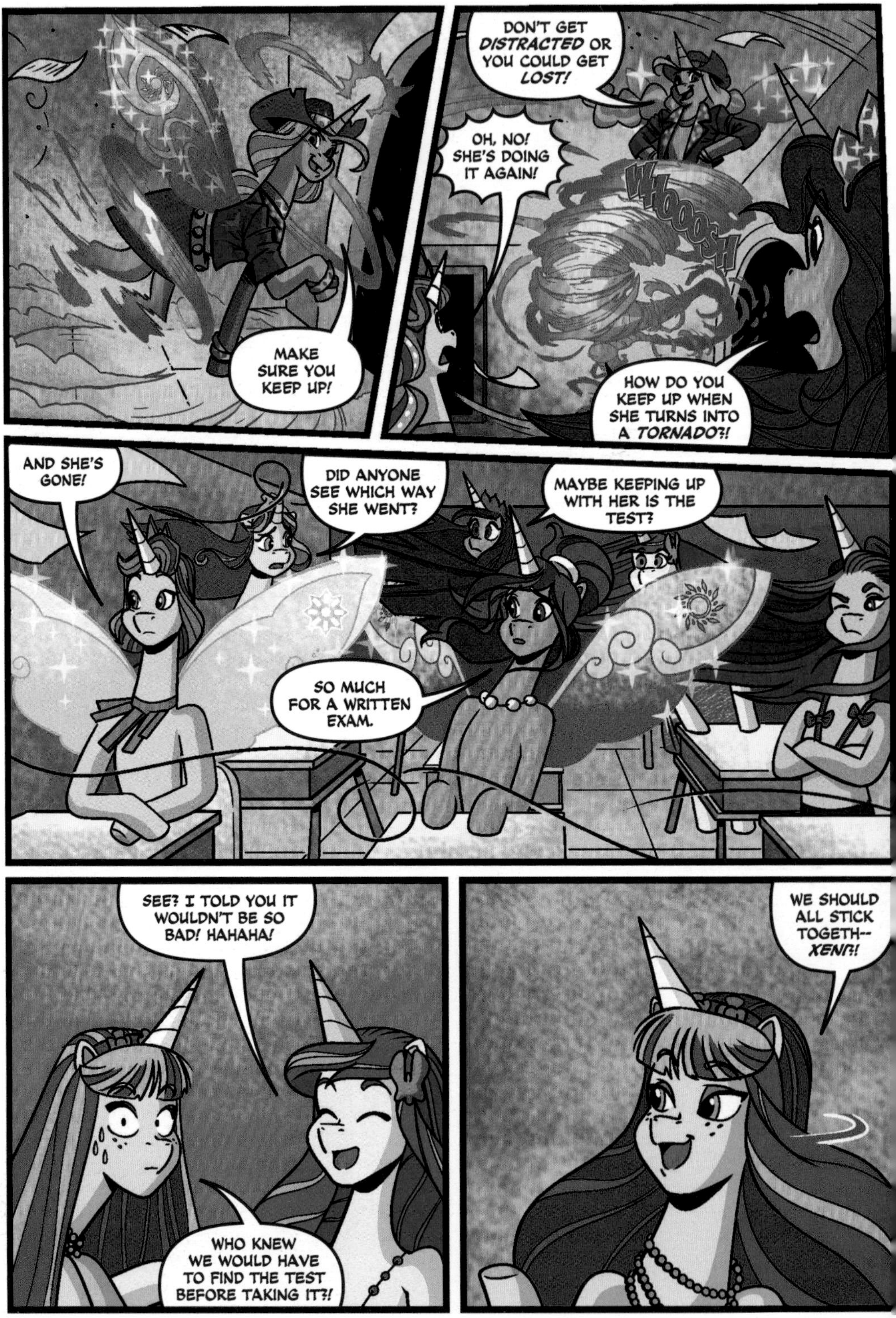
MAKE SURE YOU KEEP UP!
DON'T GET DISTRACTED OR YOU COULD GET LOST!
OH, NO! SHE'S DOING IT AGAIN!
WHOOOSH
HOW DO YOU KEEP UP WHEN SHE TURNS INTO A TORNADO?!
AND SHE'S GONE!
DID ANYONE SEE WHICH WAY SHE WENT?
MAYBE KEEPING UP WITH HER IS THE TEST?
SO MUCH FOR A WRITTEN EXAM.
SEE? I TOLD YOU IT WOULDN'T BE SO BAD! HAHAHA!
WHO KNEW WE WOULD HAVE TO FIND THE TEST BEFORE TAKING IT?!
WE SHOULD ALL STICK TOGETH-- XENI?!

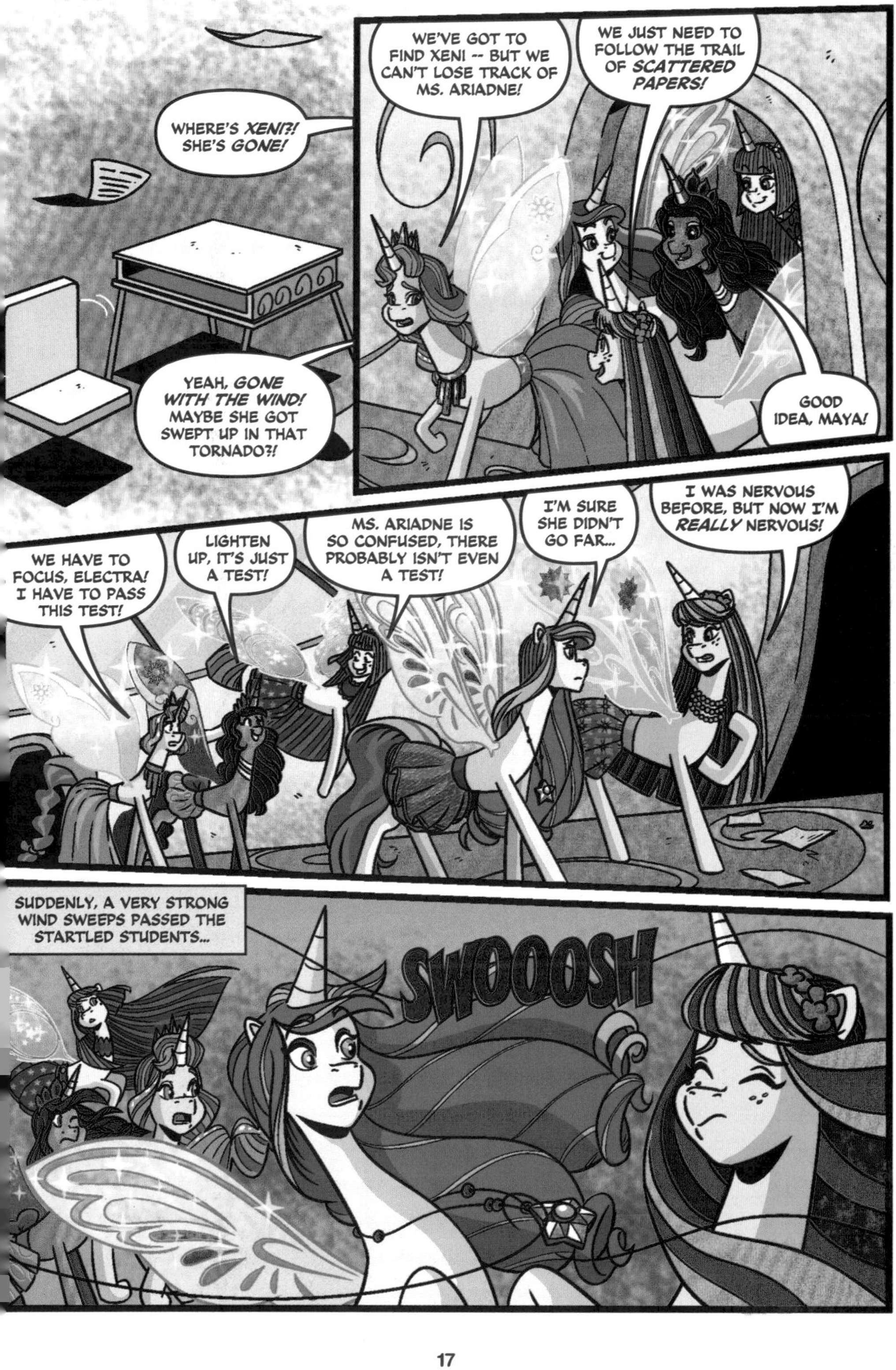
WHERE'S XENI?! SHE'S GONE!
WE'VE GOT TO FIND XENI -- BUT WE CAN'T LOSE TRACK OF MS. ARIADNE!
WE JUST NEED TO FOLLOW THE TRAIL OF SCATTERED PAPERS!
YEAH, GONE WITH THE WIND! MAYBE SHE GOT SWEPT UP IN THAT TORNADO?!
GOOD IDEA, MAYA!
WE HAVE TO FOCUS, ELECTRA! I HAVE TO PASS THIS TEST!
LIGHTEN UP, IT'S JUST A TEST!
MS. ARIADNE IS SO CONFUSED, THERE PROBABLY ISN'T EVEN A TEST!
I'M SURE SHE DIDN'T GO FAR...
I WAS NERVOUS BEFORE, BUT NOW I'M REALLY NERVOUS!
SUDDENLY, A VERY STRONG WIND SWEEPS PASSED THE STARTLED STUDENTS...
SWOOOSH

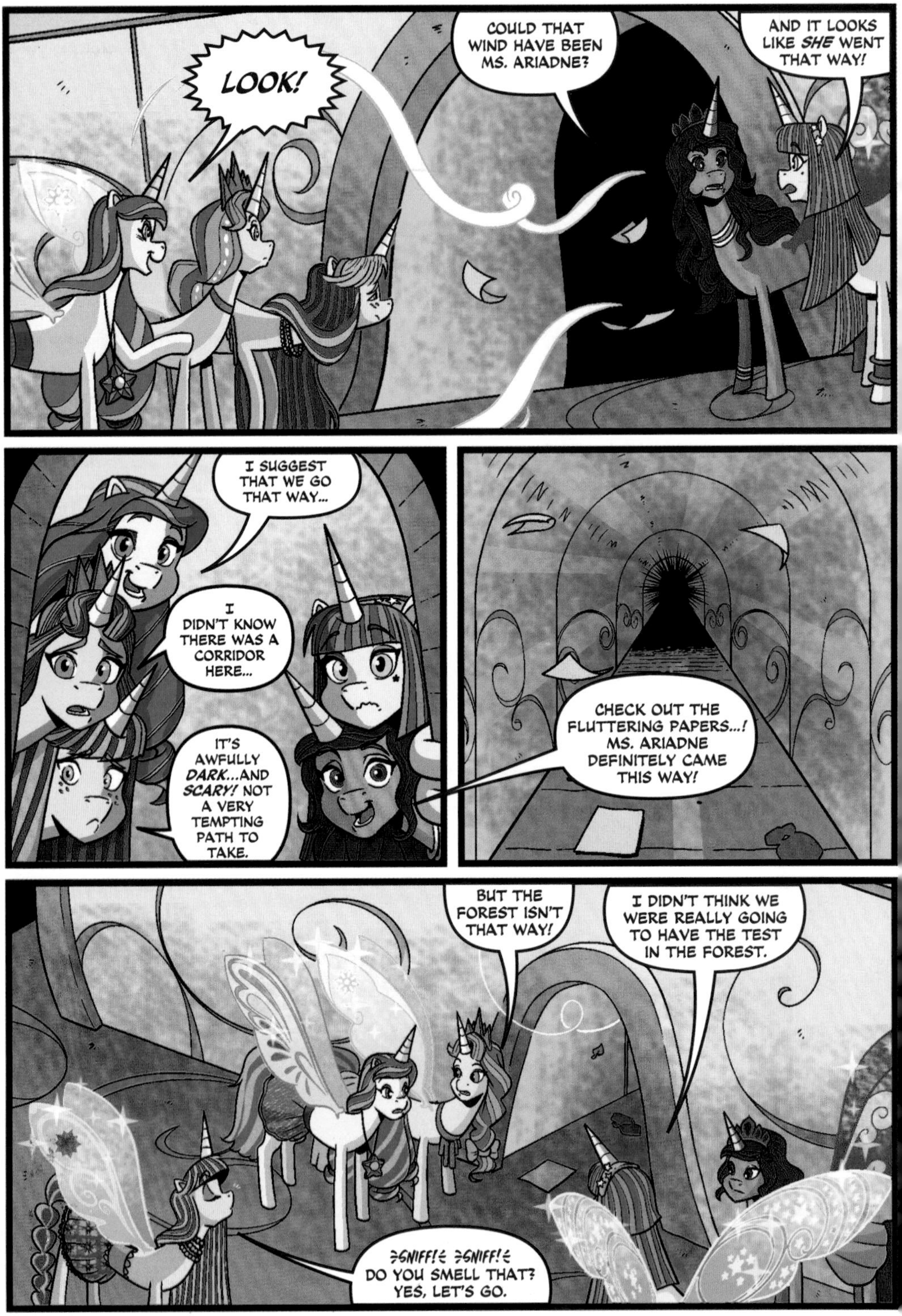
LOOK!
COULD THAT WIND HAVE BEEN MS. ARIADNE?
AND IT LOOKS LIKE SHE WENT THAT WAY!
I SUGGEST THAT WE GO THAT WAY...
I DIDN'T KNOW THERE WAS A CORRIDOR HERE...
IT'S AWFULLY DARK...AND SCARY! NOT A VERY TEMPTING PATH TO TAKE.
CHECK OUT THE FLUTTERING PAPERS...! MS. ARIADNE DEFINITELY CAME THIS WAY!
BUT THE FOREST ISN'T THAT WAY!
I DIDN'T THINK WE WERE REALLY GOING TO HAVE THE TEST IN THE FOREST.
SNIFF! SNIFF! DO YOU SMELL THAT? YES, LET'S GO.

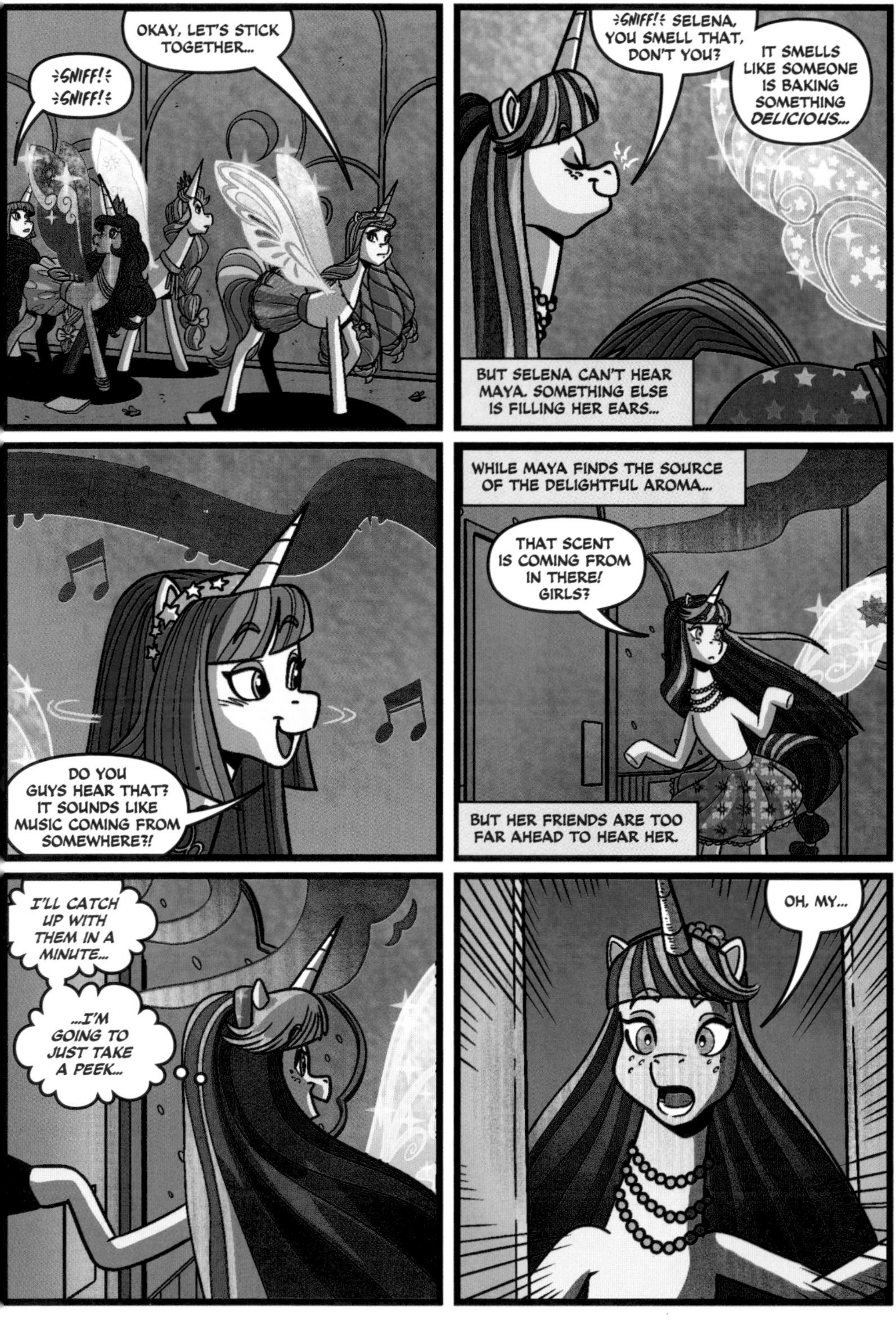
⸗SNIFF!⸗ ⸗SNIFF!⸗
OKAY, LET'S STICK TOGETHER...
⸗SNIFF!⸗ SELENA, YOU SMELL THAT, DON'T YOU?
IT SMELLS LIKE SOMEONE IS BAKING SOMETHING DELICIOUS...
BUT SELENA CAN'T HEAR MAYA. SOMETHING ELSE IS FILLING HER EARS...
DO YOU GUYS HEAR THAT? IT SOUNDS LIKE MUSIC COMING FROM SOMEWHERE?!
WHILE MAYA FINDS THE SOURCE OF THE DELIGHTFUL AROMA...
THAT SCENT IS COMING FROM IN THERE! GIRLS?
BUT HER FRIENDS ARE TOO FAR AHEAD TO HEAR HER.
I'LL CATCH UP WITH THEM IN A MINUTE...
...I'M GOING TO JUST TAKE A PEEK...
OH, MY...

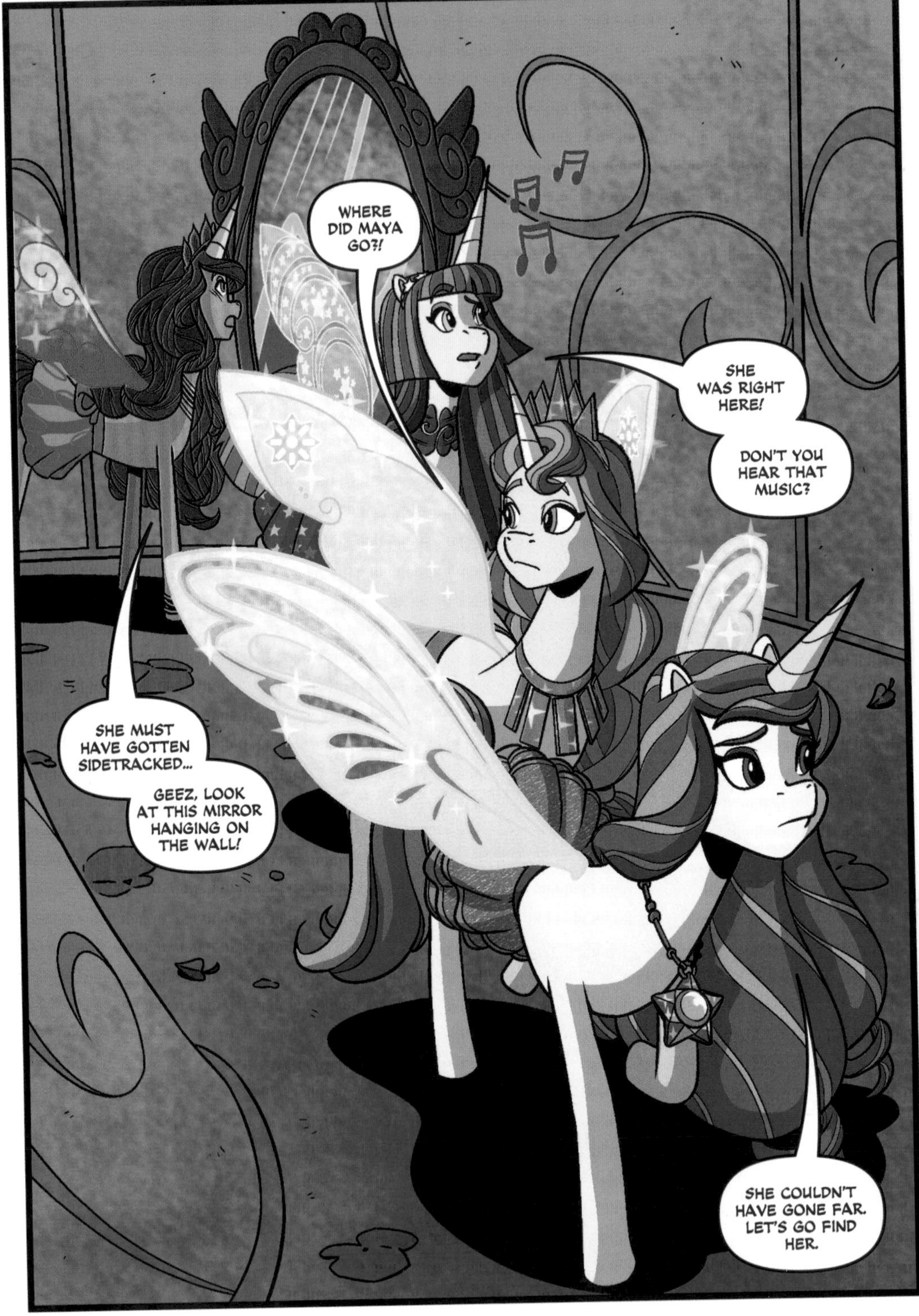
WHERE DID MAYA GO?!
SHE WAS RIGHT HERE!
DON'T YOU HEAR THAT MUSIC?
SHE MUST HAVE GOTTEN SIDETRACKED...
GEEZ, LOOK AT THIS MIRROR HANGING ON THE WALL!
SHE COULDN'T HAVE GONE FAR. LET'S GO FIND HER.

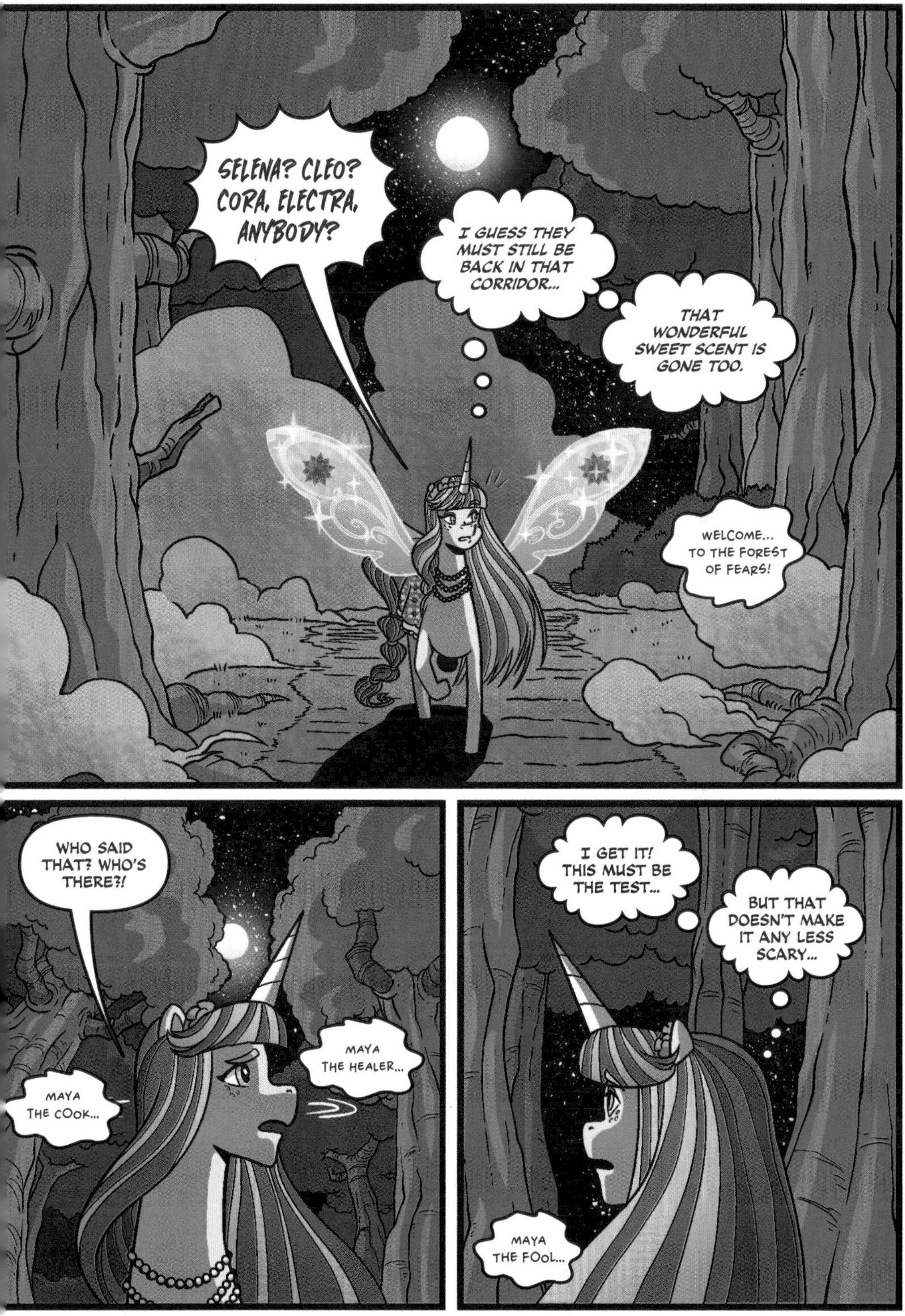
SELENA? CLEO? CORA, ELECTRA, ANYBODY?
I GUESS THEY MUST STILL BE BACK IN THAT CORRIDOR...
THAT WONDERFUL SWEET SCENT IS GONE TOO.
WELCOME... TO THE FOREST OF FEARS!
WHO SAID THAT? WHO'S THERE?!
MAYA THE COOK...
MAYA THE HEALER...
I GET IT! THIS MUST BE THE TEST...
BUT THAT DOESN'T MAKE IT ANY LESS SCARY...
MAYA THE FOOL...

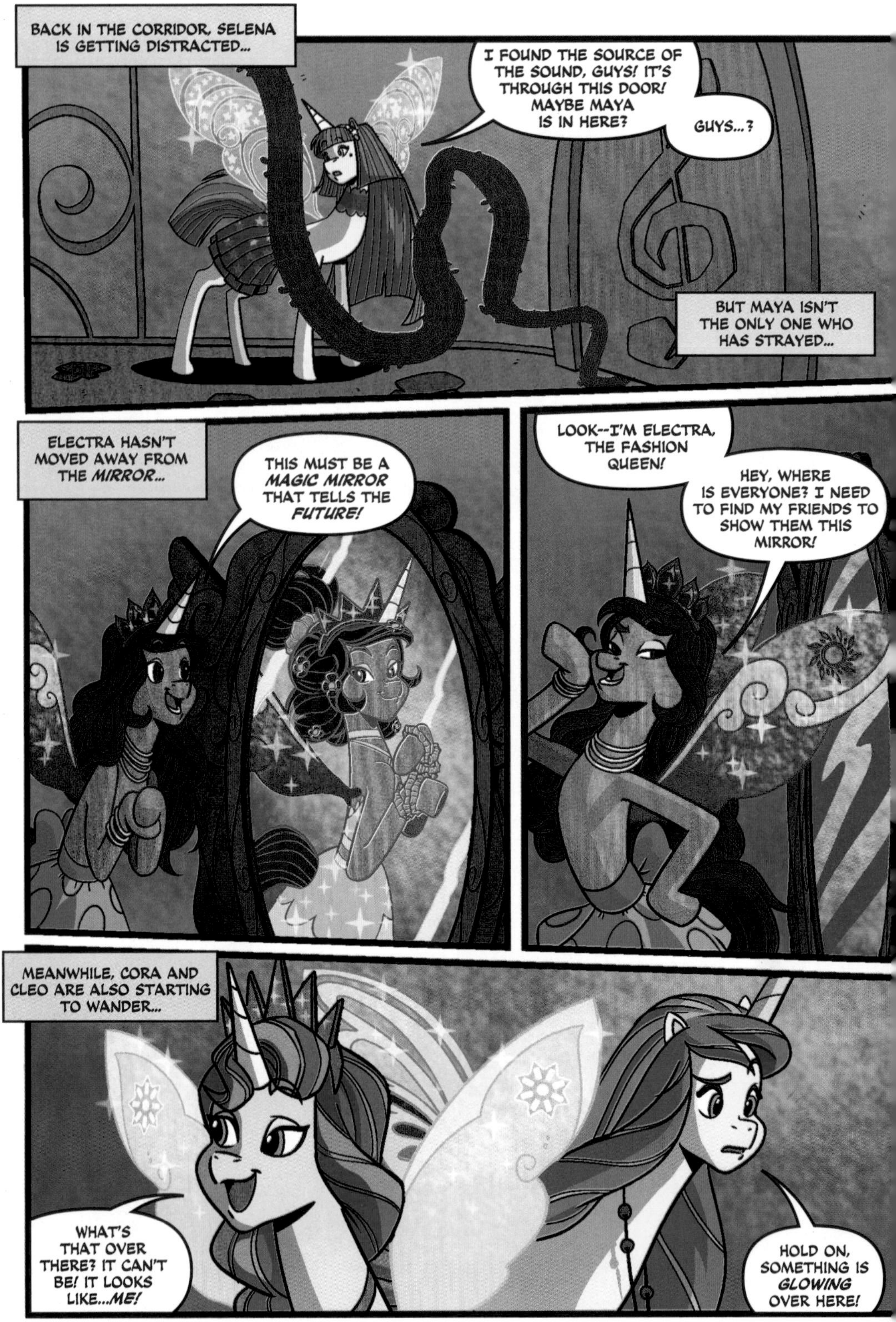
BACK IN THE CORRIDOR, SELENA IS GETTING DISTRACTED...
I FOUND THE SOURCE OF THE SOUND, GUYS! IT'S THROUGH THIS DOOR! MAYBE MAYA IS IN HERE?
GUYS...?
BUT MAYA ISN'T THE ONLY ONE WHO HAS STRAYED...
ELECTRA HASN'T MOVED AWAY FROM THE *MIRROR*...
THIS MUST BE A *MAGIC MIRROR* THAT TELLS THE *FUTURE!*
LOOK--I'M ELECTRA, THE FASHION QUEEN!
HEY, WHERE IS EVERYONE? I NEED TO FIND MY FRIENDS TO SHOW THEM THIS MIRROR!
MEANWHILE, CORA AND CLEO ARE ALSO STARTING TO WANDER...
WHAT'S THAT OVER THERE? IT CAN'T BE! IT LOOKS LIKE...*ME!*
HOLD ON, SOMETHING IS *GLOWING* OVER HERE!

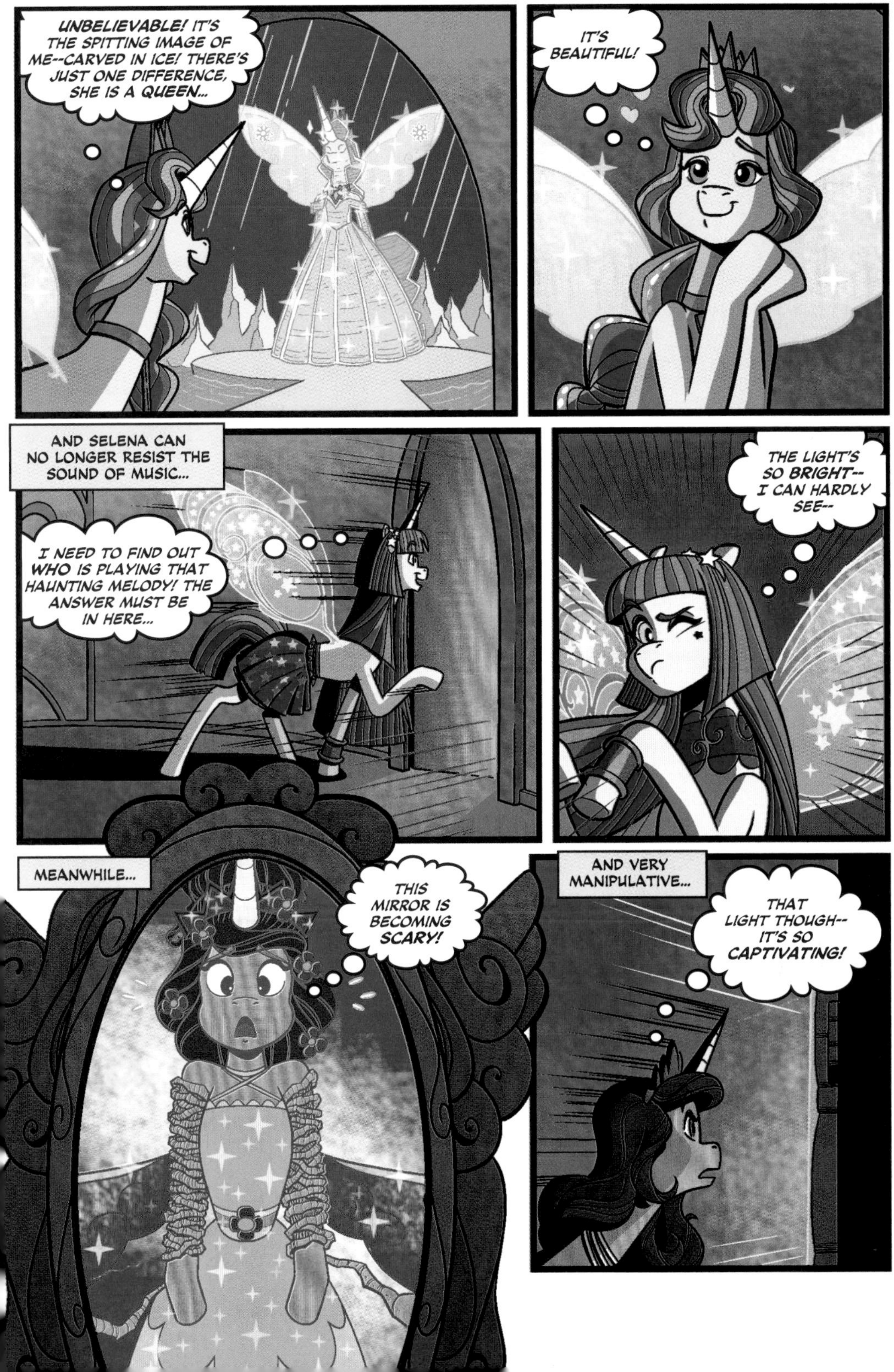
UNBELIEVABLE! IT'S THE SPITTING IMAGE OF ME--CARVED IN ICE! THERE'S JUST ONE DIFFERENCE, SHE IS A QUEEN...
IT'S BEAUTIFUL!
AND SELENA CAN NO LONGER RESIST THE SOUND OF MUSIC...
I NEED TO FIND OUT WHO IS PLAYING THAT HAUNTING MELODY! THE ANSWER MUST BE IN HERE...
THE LIGHT'S SO BRIGHT-- I CAN HARDLY SEE--
MEANWHILE...
THIS MIRROR IS BECOMING SCARY!
AND VERY MANIPULATIVE...
THAT LIGHT THOUGH-- IT'S SO CAPTIVATING!

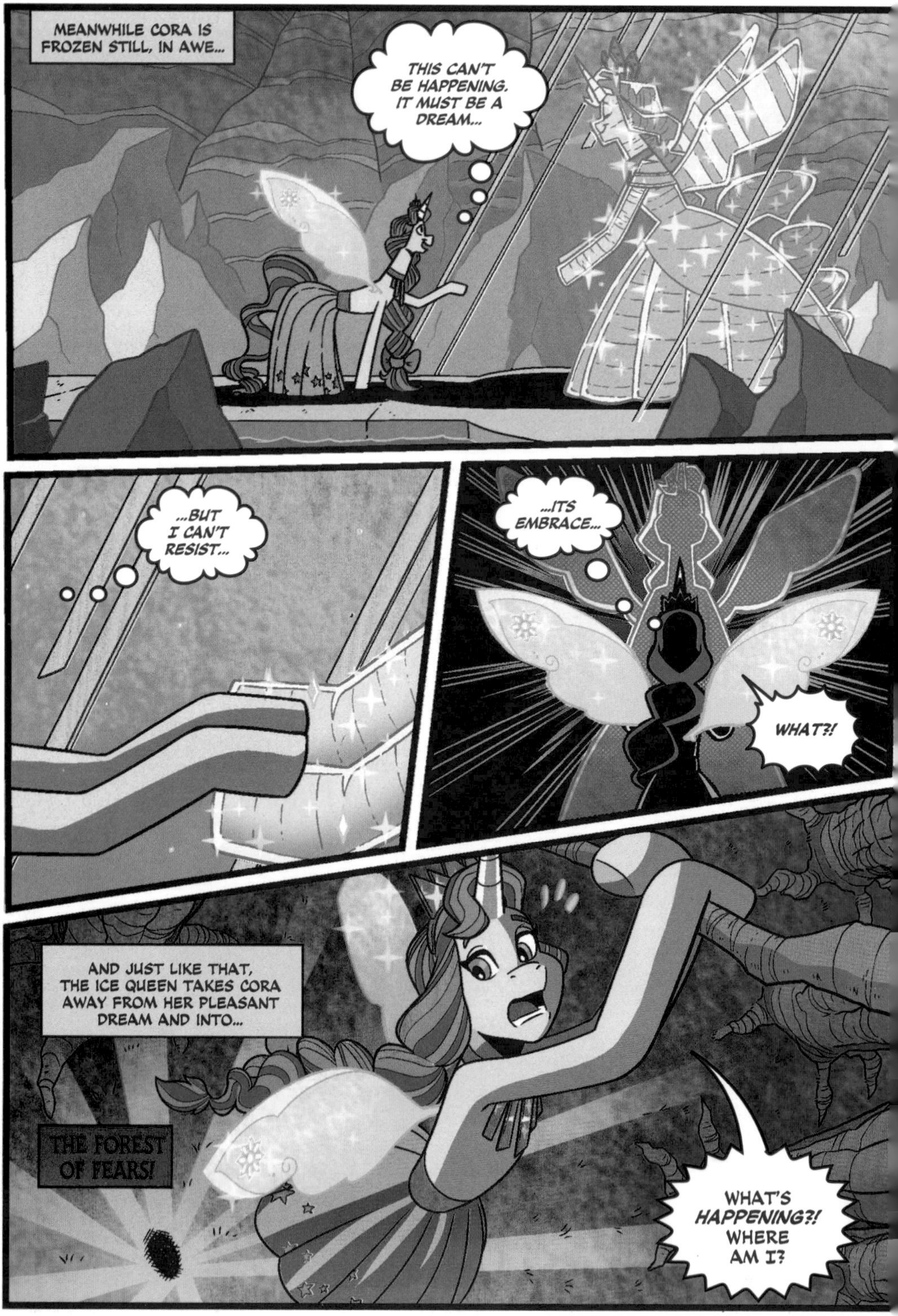
MEANWHILE CORA IS FROZEN STILL, IN AWE...
THIS CAN'T BE HAPPENING. IT MUST BE A DREAM...
...BUT I CAN'T RESIST...
...ITS EMBRACE...
WHAT?!
AND JUST LIKE THAT, THE ICE QUEEN TAKES CORA AWAY FROM HER PLEASANT DREAM AND INTO...
THE FOREST OF FEARS!
WHAT'S HAPPENING?! WHERE AM I?

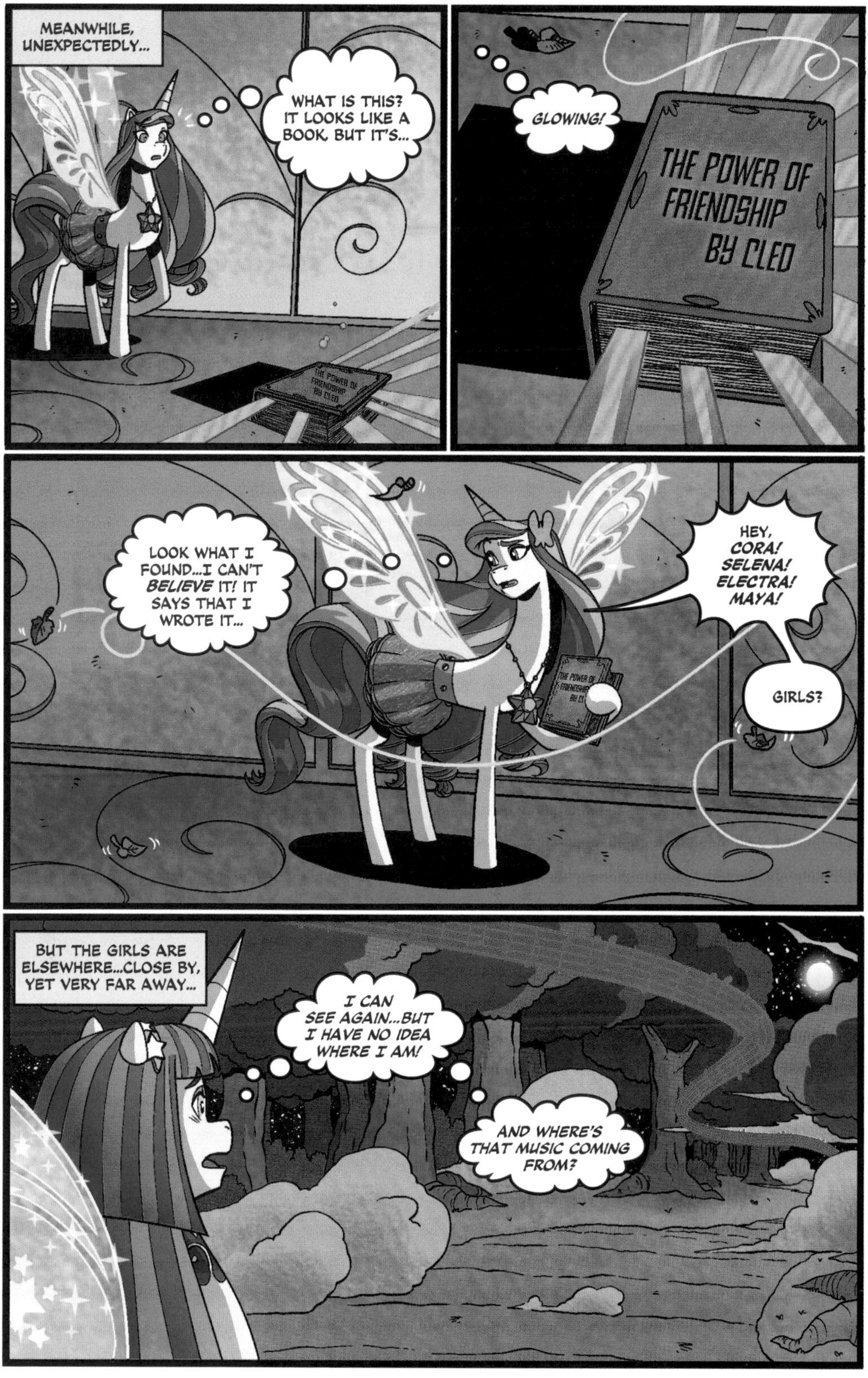
MEANWHILE, UNEXPECTEDLY...
WHAT IS THIS? IT LOOKS LIKE A BOOK, BUT IT'S...
GLOWING!
THE POWER OF FRIENDSHIP BY CLEO
LOOK WHAT I FOUND...I CAN'T BELIEVE IT! IT SAYS THAT I WROTE IT...
HEY, CORA! SELENA! ELECTRA! MAYA!
GIRLS?
BUT THE GIRLS ARE ELSEWHERE...CLOSE BY, YET VERY FAR AWAY...
I CAN SEE AGAIN...BUT I HAVE NO IDEA WHERE I AM!
AND WHERE'S THAT MUSIC COMING FROM?

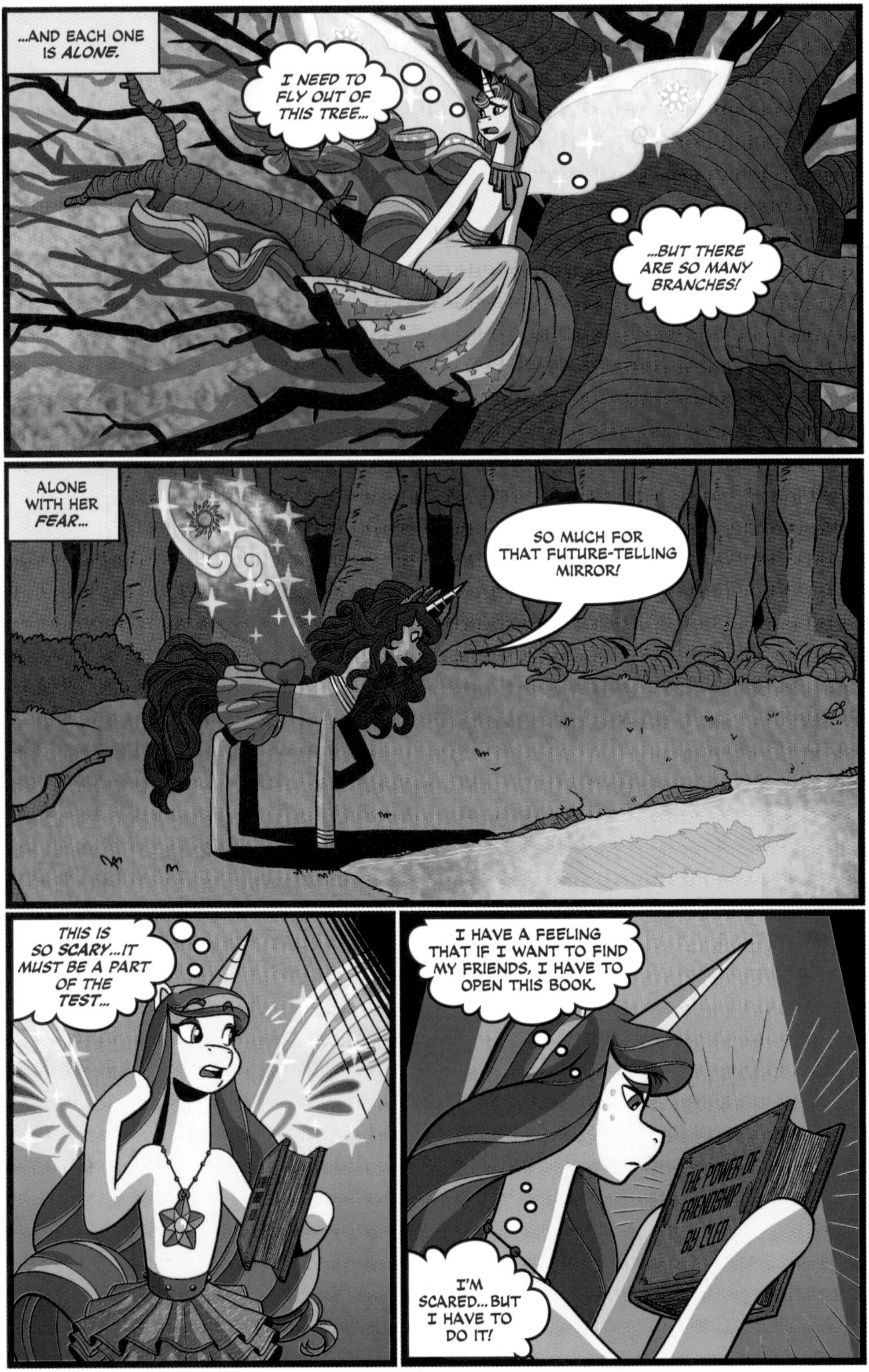
...AND EACH ONE IS ALONE.
I NEED TO FLY OUT OF THIS TREE...
...BUT THERE ARE SO MANY BRANCHES!
ALONE WITH HER FEAR...
SO MUCH FOR THAT FUTURE-TELLING MIRROR!
THIS IS SO SCARY...IT MUST BE A PART OF THE TEST...
I HAVE A FEELING THAT IF I WANT TO FIND MY FRIENDS, I HAVE TO OPEN THIS BOOK.
THE POWER OF FRIENDSHIP BY CLEO
I'M SCARED... BUT I HAVE TO DO IT!

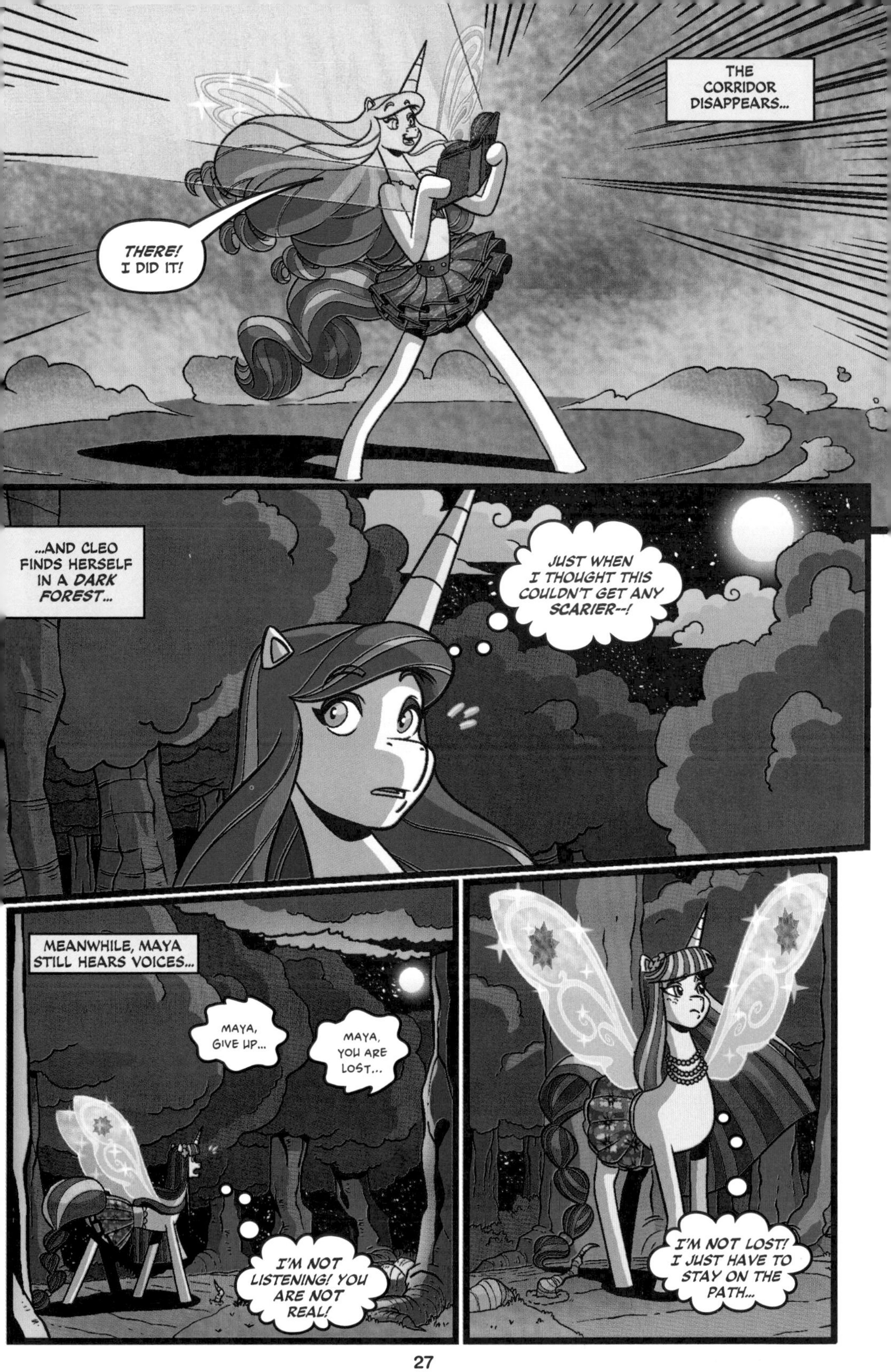
THE CORRIDOR DISAPPEARS...
THERE! I DID IT!
...AND CLEO FINDS HERSELF IN A DARK FOREST...
JUST WHEN I THOUGHT THIS COULDN'T GET ANY SCARIER--!
MEANWHILE, MAYA STILL HEARS VOICES...
MAYA, GIVE UP...
MAYA, YOU ARE LOST...
I'M NOT LISTENING! YOU ARE NOT REAL!
I'M NOT LOST! I JUST HAVE TO STAY ON THE PATH...

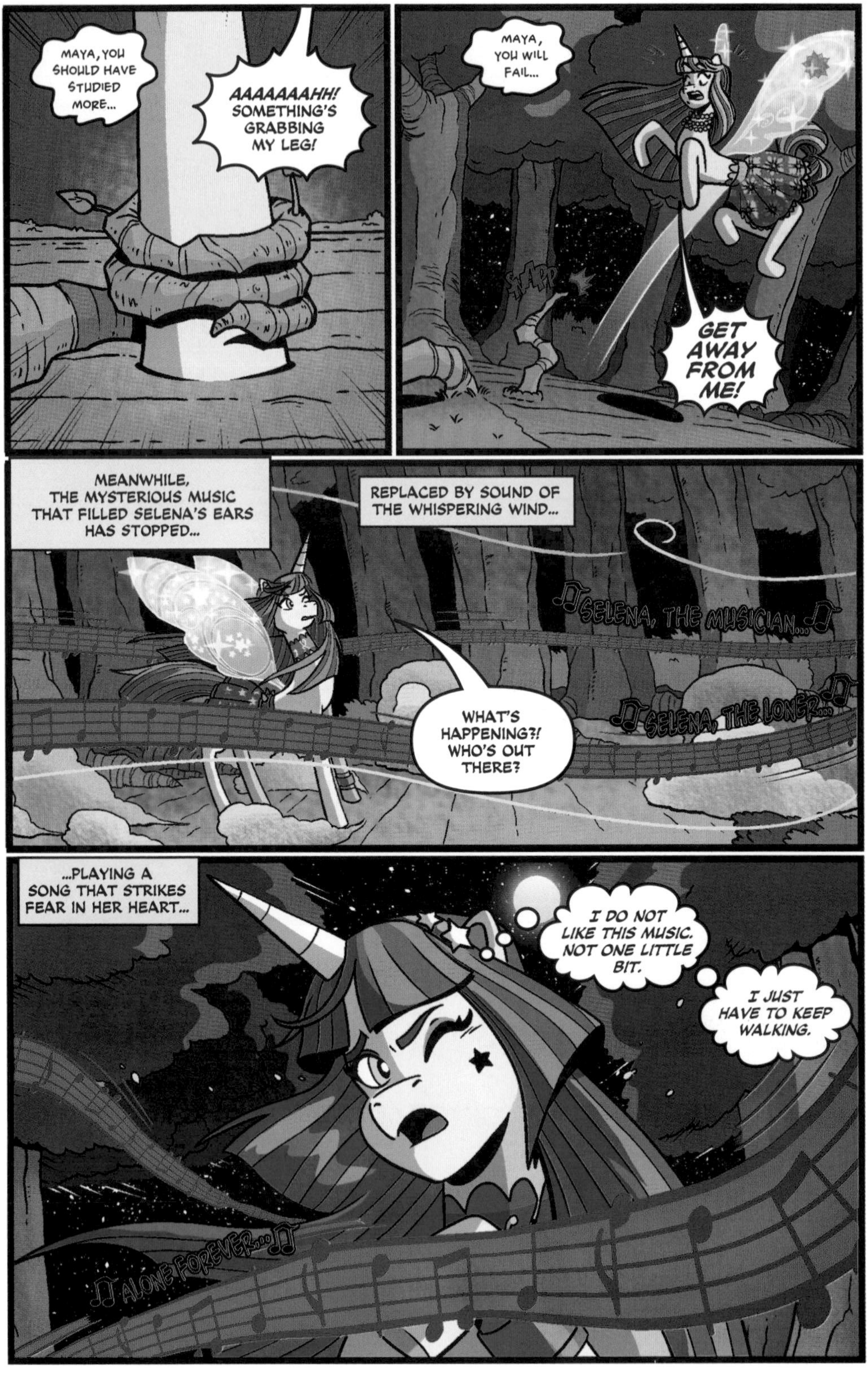
MAYA, YOU SHOULD HAVE STUDIED MORE...
AAAAAAAHH! SOMETHING'S GRABBING MY LEG!
MAYA, YOU WILL FAIL...
SNAPP
GET AWAY FROM ME!
MEANWHILE, THE MYSTERIOUS MUSIC THAT FILLED SELENA'S EARS HAS STOPPED...
REPLACED BY SOUND OF THE WHISPERING WIND...
SELENA, THE MUSICIAN...
SELENA, THE LONER...
WHAT'S HAPPENING?! WHO'S OUT THERE?
...PLAYING A SONG THAT STRIKES FEAR IN HER HEART...
I DO NOT LIKE THIS MUSIC. NOT ONE LITTLE BIT.
I JUST HAVE TO KEEP WALKING.
ALONE FOREVER...

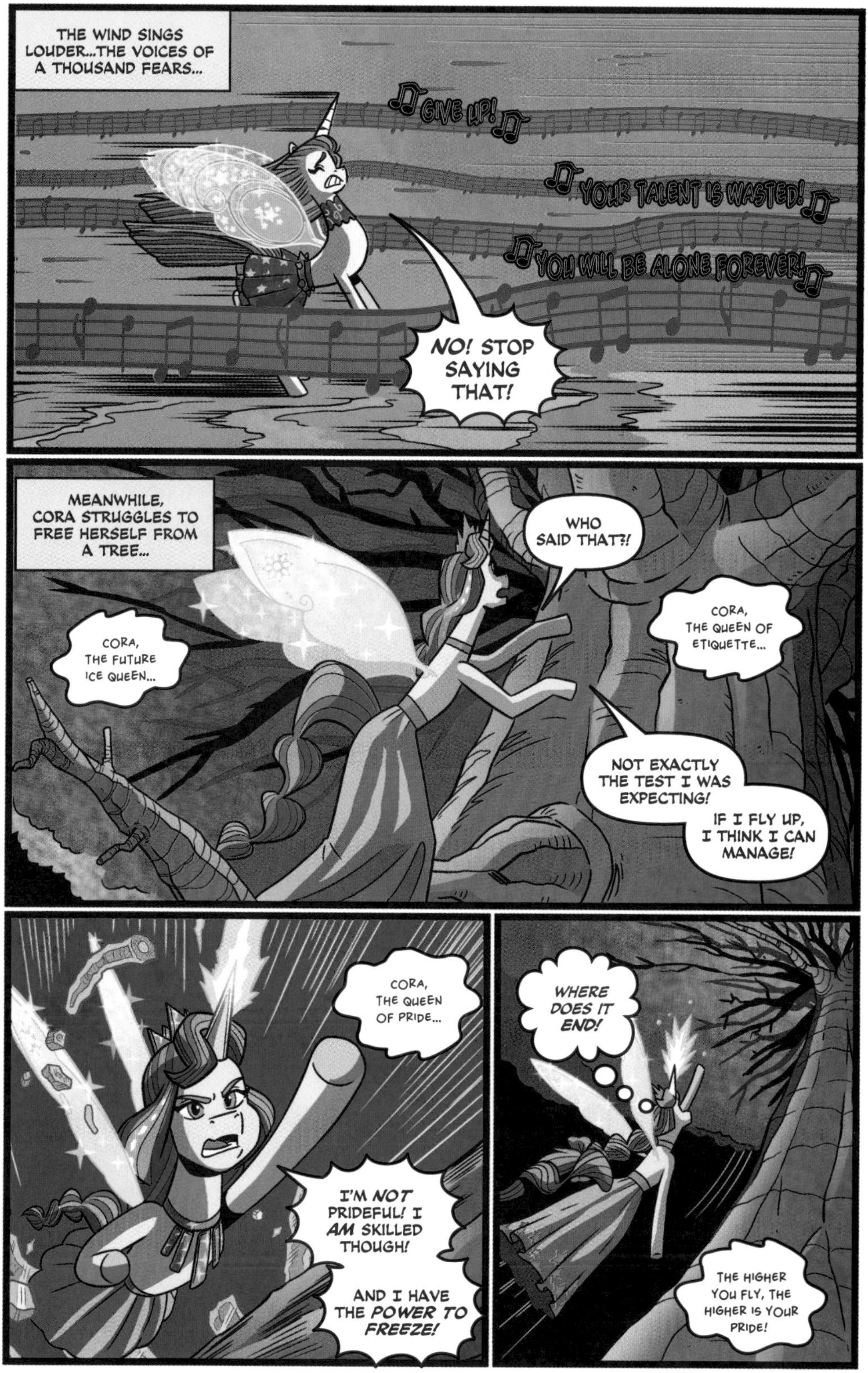
THE WIND SINGS LOUDER...THE VOICES OF A THOUSAND FEARS...
♫ GIVE UP! ♫
♫ YOUR TALENT IS WASTED! ♫
♫ YOU WILL BE ALONE FOREVER! ♫
NO! STOP SAYING THAT!
MEANWHILE, CORA STRUGGLES TO FREE HERSELF FROM A TREE...
WHO SAID THAT?!
CORA, THE FUTURE ICE QUEEN...
CORA, THE QUEEN OF ETIQUETTE...
NOT EXACTLY THE TEST I WAS EXPECTING!
IF I FLY UP, I THINK I CAN MANAGE!
CORA, THE QUEEN OF PRIDE...
I'M NOT PRIDEFUL! I AM SKILLED THOUGH!
AND I HAVE THE POWER TO FREEZE!
WHERE DOES IT END!
THE HIGHER YOU FLY, THE HIGHER IS YOUR PRIDE!

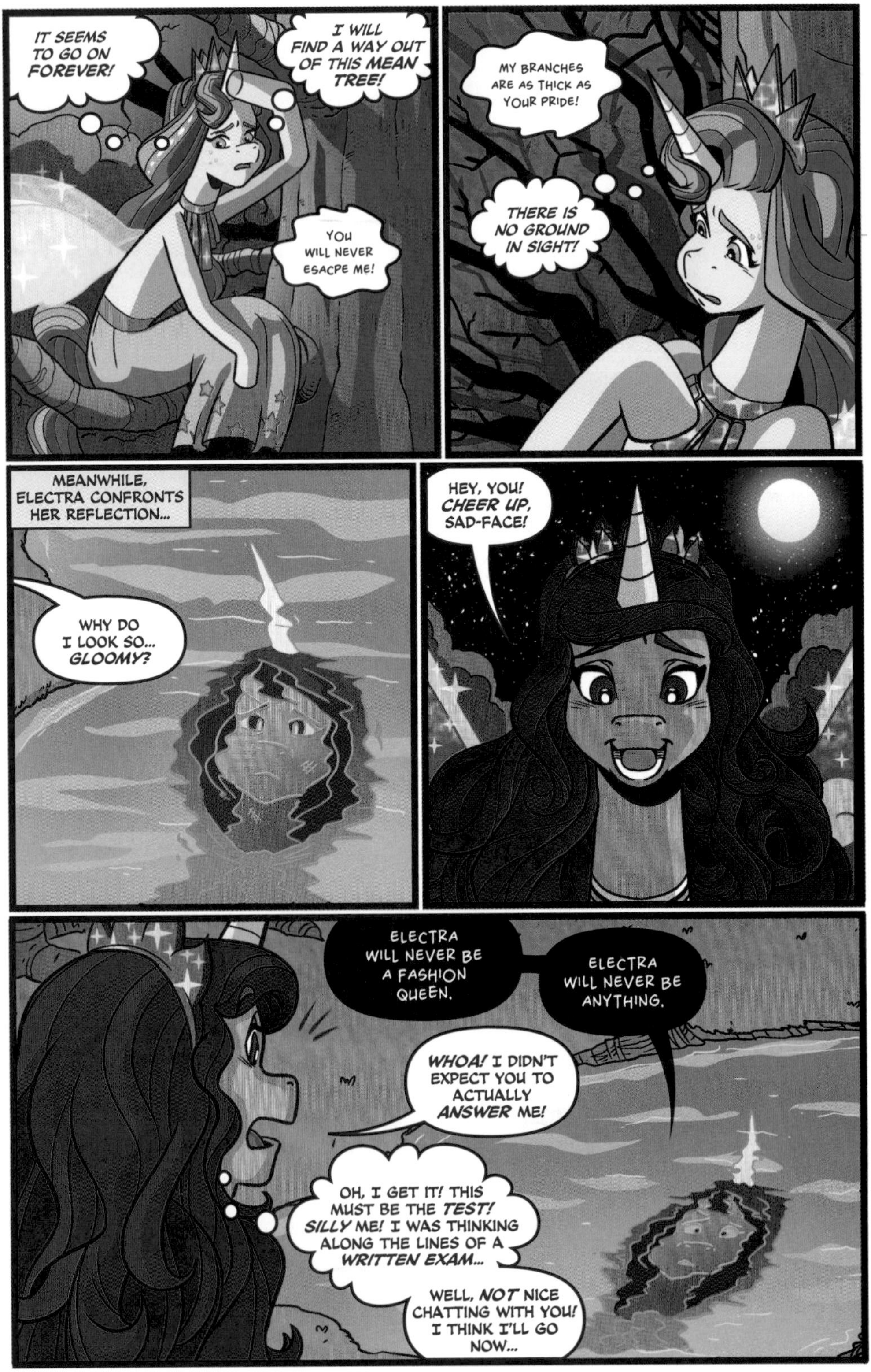
IT SEEMS TO GO ON FOREVER!
I WILL FIND A WAY OUT OF THIS MEAN TREE!
YOU WILL NEVER ESACPE ME!
MY BRANCHES ARE AS THICK AS YOUR PRIDE!
THERE IS NO GROUND IN SIGHT!
MEANWHILE, ELECTRA CONFRONTS HER REFLECTION...
WHY DO I LOOK SO... GLOOMY?
HEY, YOU! CHEER UP, SAD-FACE!
ELECTRA WILL NEVER BE A FASHION QUEEN.
ELECTRA WILL NEVER BE ANYTHING.
WHOA! I DIDN'T EXPECT YOU TO ACTUALLY ANSWER ME!
OH, I GET IT! THIS MUST BE THE TEST! SILLY ME! I WAS THINKING ALONG THE LINES OF A WRITTEN EXAM...
WELL, NOT NICE CHATTING WITH YOU! I THINK I'LL GO NOW...

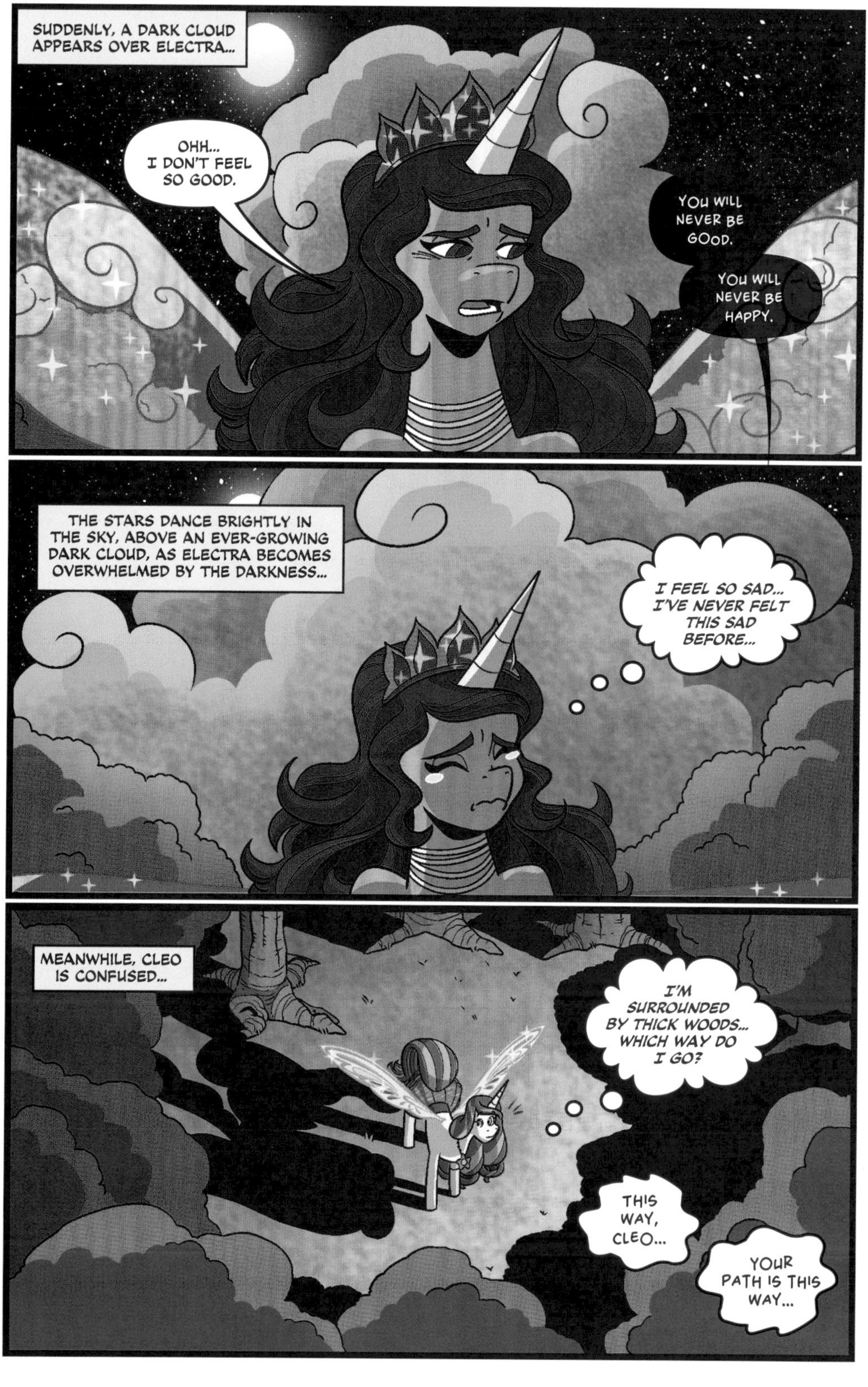
SUDDENLY, A DARK CLOUD APPEARS OVER ELECTRA...
OHH... I DON'T FEEL SO GOOD.
YOU WILL NEVER BE GOOD.
YOU WILL NEVER BE HAPPY.
THE STARS DANCE BRIGHTLY IN THE SKY, ABOVE AN EVER-GROWING DARK CLOUD, AS ELECTRA BECOMES OVERWHELMED BY THE DARKNESS...
I FEEL SO SAD... I'VE NEVER FELT THIS SAD BEFORE...
MEANWHILE, CLEO IS CONFUSED...
I'M SURROUNDED BY THICK WOODS... WHICH WAY DO I GO?
THIS WAY, CLEO...
YOUR PATH IS THIS WAY...

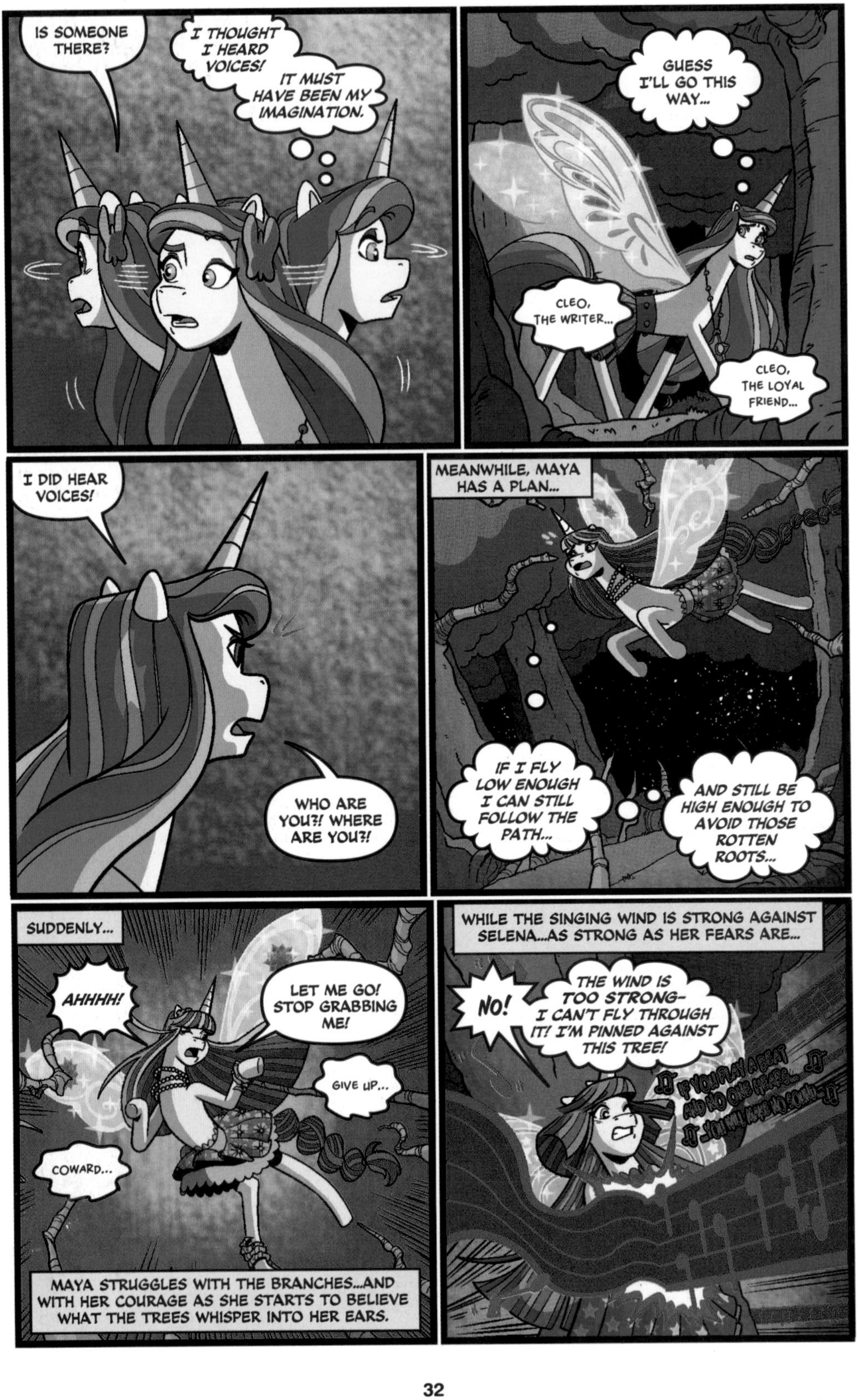
IS SOMEONE THERE?
I THOUGHT I HEARD VOICES!
IT MUST HAVE BEEN MY IMAGINATION.
GUESS I'LL GO THIS WAY...
CLEO, THE WRITER...
CLEO, THE LOYAL FRIEND...
I DID HEAR VOICES!
WHO ARE YOU?! WHERE ARE YOU?!
MEANWHILE, MAYA HAS A PLAN...
IF I FLY LOW ENOUGH I CAN STILL FOLLOW THE PATH...
AND STILL BE HIGH ENOUGH TO AVOID THOSE ROTTEN ROOTS...
SUDDENLY...
AHHHH!
LET ME GO! STOP GRABBING ME!
GIVE UP...
COWARD...
MAYA STRUGGLES WITH THE BRANCHES...AND WITH HER COURAGE AS SHE STARTS TO BELIEVE WHAT THE TREES WHISPER INTO HER EARS.
WHILE THE SINGING WIND IS STRONG AGAINST SELENA...AS STRONG AS HER FEARS ARE...
NO!
THE WIND IS TOO STRONG– I CAN'T FLY THROUGH IT! I'M PINNED AGAINST THIS TREE!
IF YOU PLAY A BEAT AND NO ONE HEARS...
...YOU WILL MAKE NO SOUND...

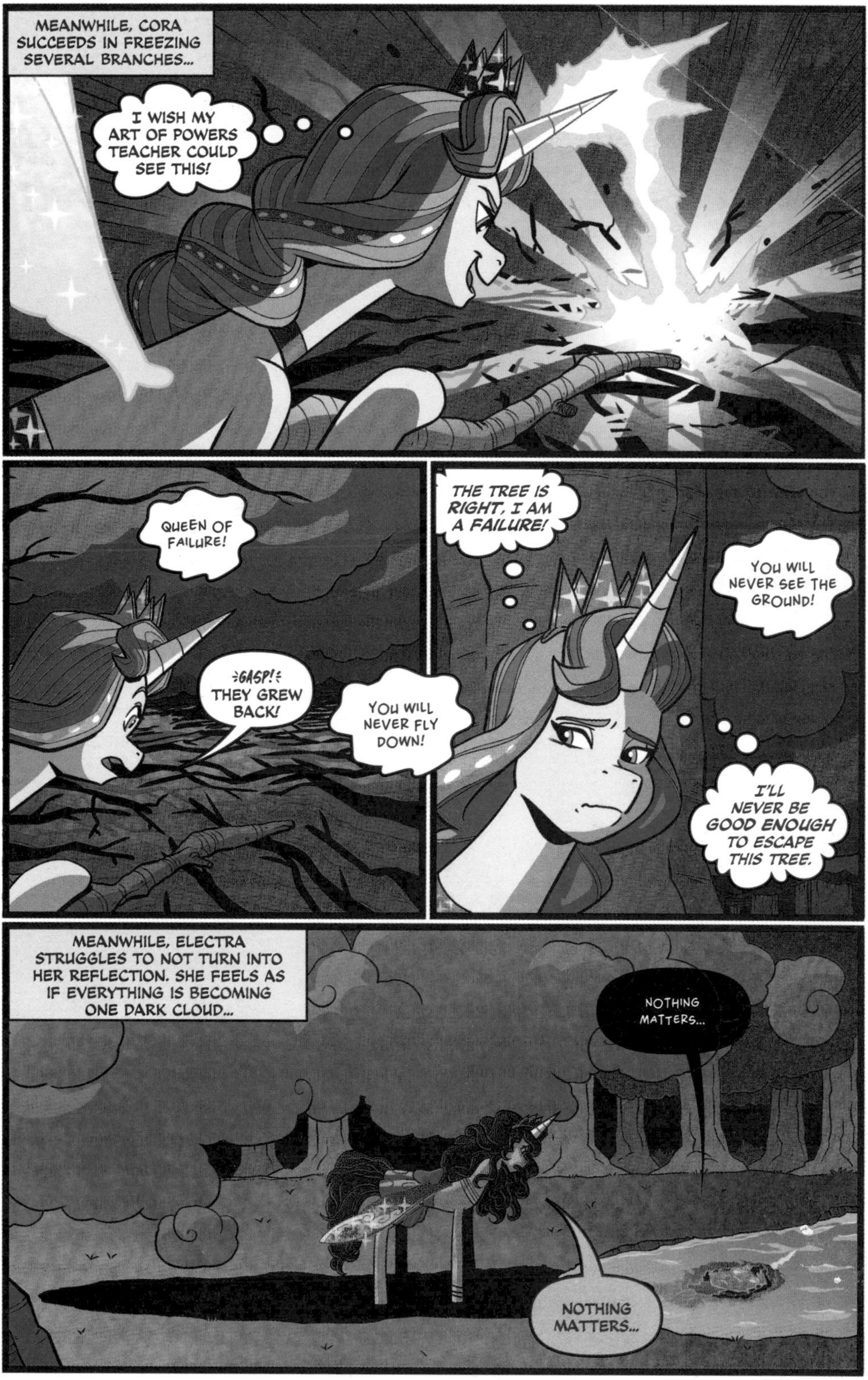

MEANWHILE, CORA SUCCEEDS IN FREEZING SEVERAL BRANCHES...
I WISH MY ART OF POWERS TEACHER COULD SEE THIS!
QUEEN OF FAILURE!
⚡GASP!⚡ THEY GREW BACK!
YOU WILL NEVER FLY DOWN!
THE TREE IS RIGHT, I AM A FAILURE!
YOU WILL NEVER SEE THE GROUND!
I'LL NEVER BE GOOD ENOUGH TO ESCAPE THIS TREE.
MEANWHILE, ELECTRA STRUGGLES TO NOT TURN INTO HER REFLECTION. SHE FEELS AS IF EVERYTHING IS BECOMING ONE DARK CLOUD...
NOTHING MATTERS...
NOTHING MATTERS...

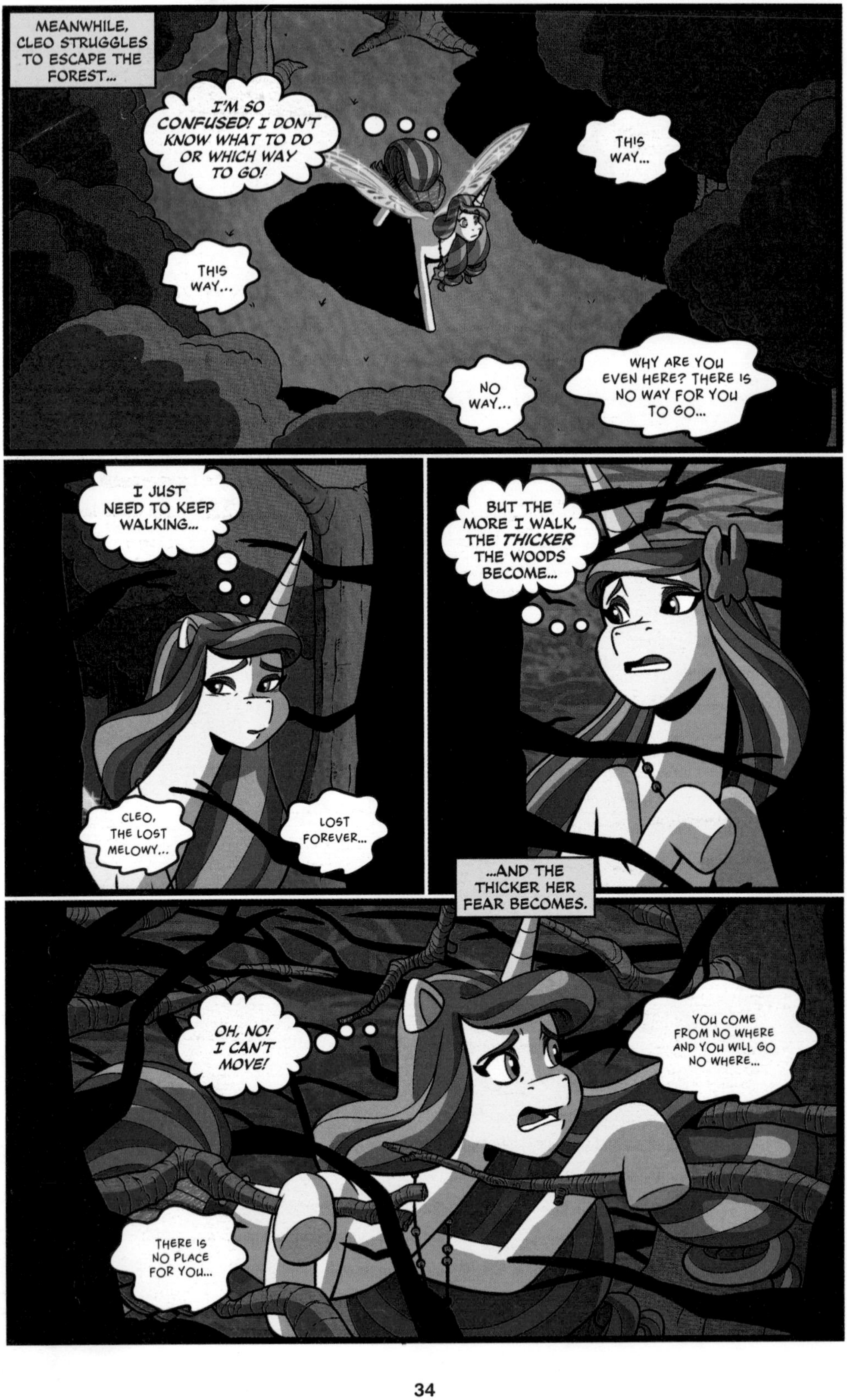
MEANWHILE, CLEO STRUGGLES TO ESCAPE THE FOREST...
I'M SO CONFUSED! I DON'T KNOW WHAT TO DO OR WHICH WAY TO GO!
THIS WAY...
THIS WAY...
NO WAY...
WHY ARE YOU EVEN HERE? THERE IS NO WAY FOR YOU TO GO...
I JUST NEED TO KEEP WALKING...
CLEO, THE LOST MELOWY...
LOST FOREVER...
BUT THE MORE I WALK, THE THICKER THE WOODS BECOME...
...AND THE THICKER HER FEAR BECOMES.
OH, NO! I CAN'T MOVE!
YOU COME FROM NO WHERE AND YOU WILL GO NO WHERE...
THERE IS NO PLACE FOR YOU...

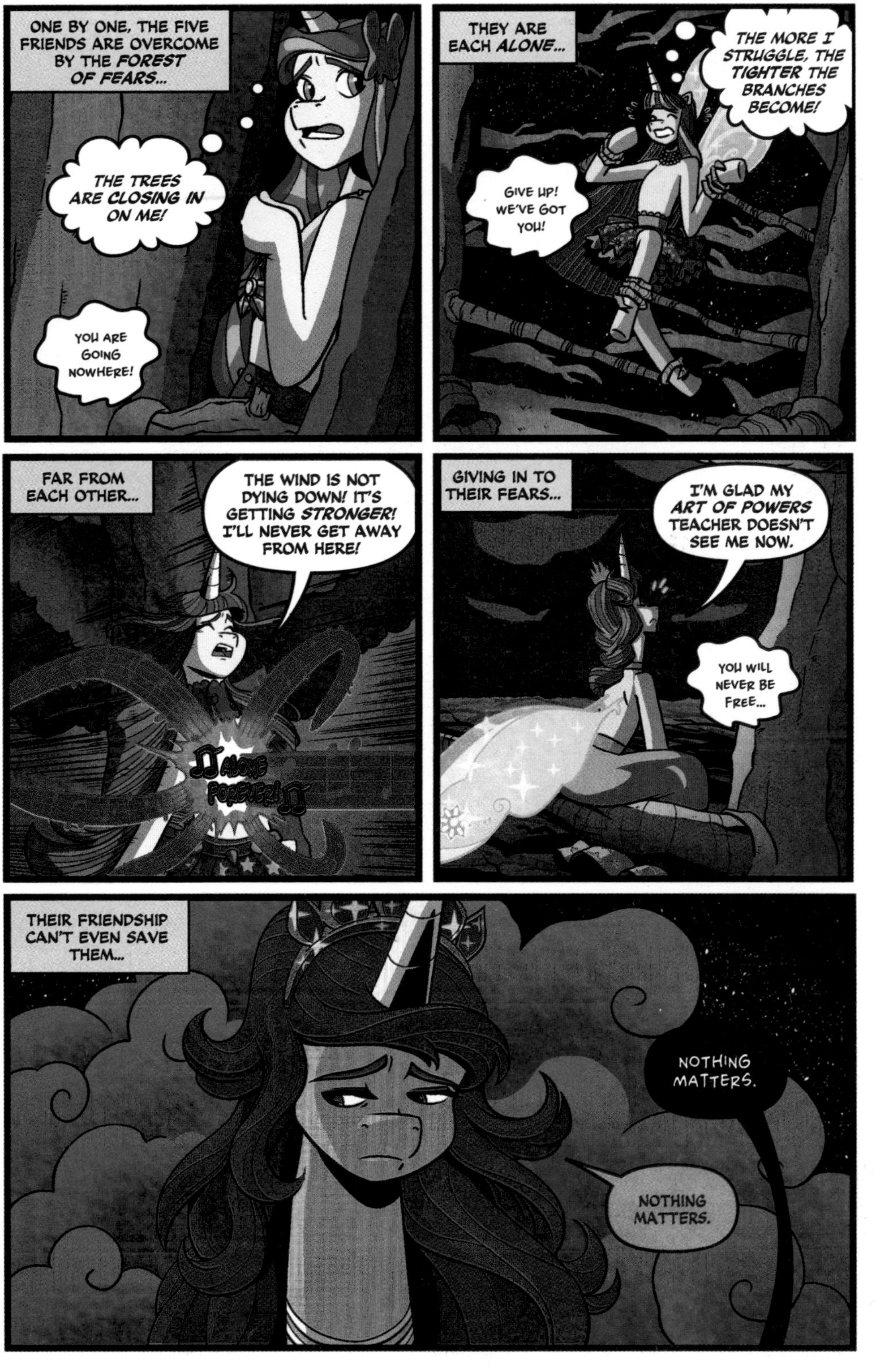
ONE BY ONE, THE FIVE FRIENDS ARE OVERCOME BY THE FOREST OF FEARS...
THE TREES ARE CLOSING IN ON ME!
YOU ARE GOING NOWHERE!
THEY ARE EACH ALONE...
THE MORE I STRUGGLE, THE TIGHTER THE BRANCHES BECOME!
GIVE UP! WE'VE GOT YOU!
FAR FROM EACH OTHER...
THE WIND IS NOT DYING DOWN! IT'S GETTING STRONGER! I'LL NEVER GET AWAY FROM HERE!
ALONE FOREVER!
GIVING IN TO THEIR FEARS...
I'M GLAD MY ART OF POWERS TEACHER DOESN'T SEE ME NOW.
YOU WILL NEVER BE FREE...
THEIR FRIENDSHIP CAN'T EVEN SAVE THEM...
NOTHING MATTERS.
NOTHING MATTERS.

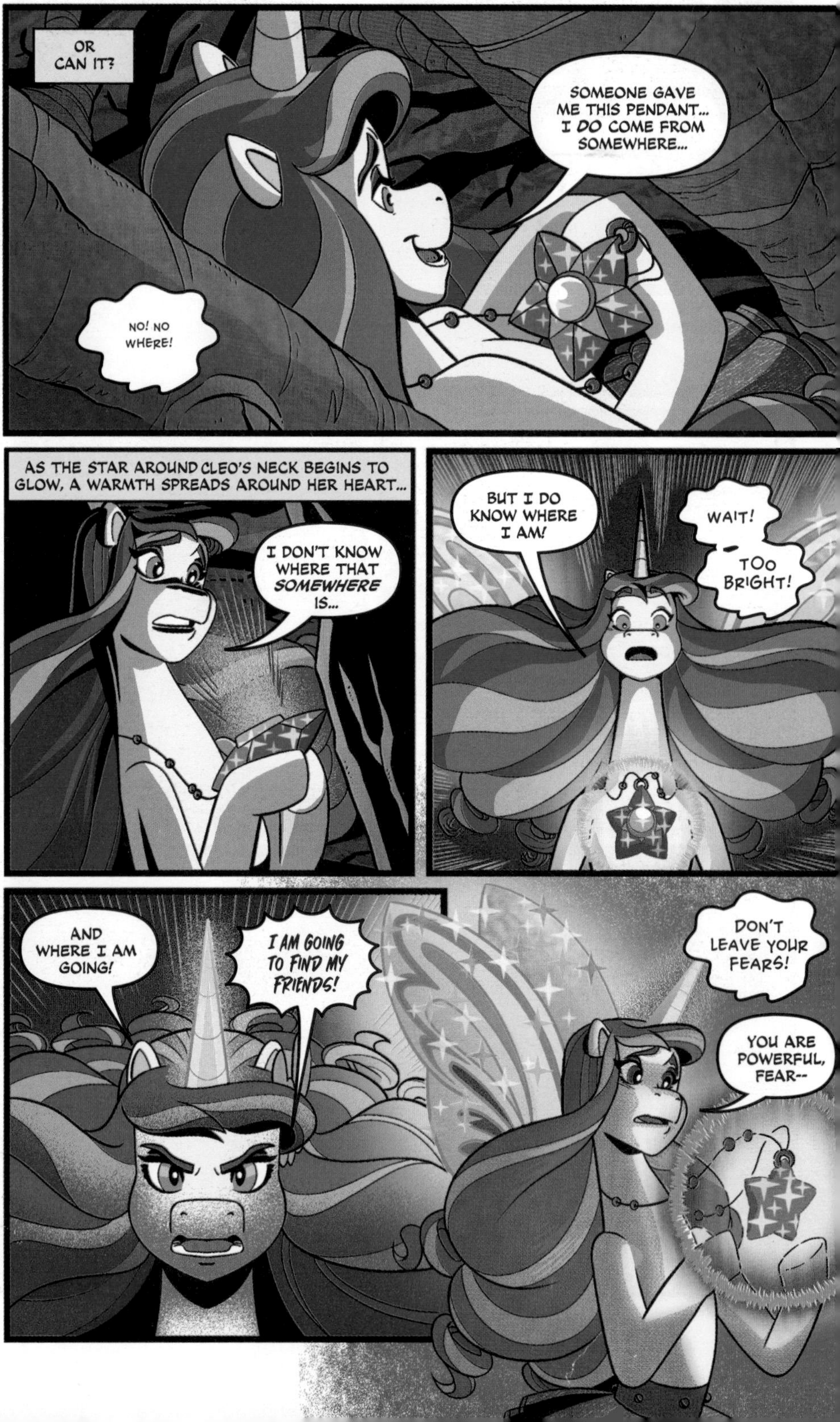
OR CAN IT?
SOMEONE GAVE ME THIS PENDANT... I DO COME FROM SOMEWHERE...
NO! NO WHERE!
AS THE STAR AROUND CLEO'S NECK BEGINS TO GLOW, A WARMTH SPREADS AROUND HER HEART...
I DON'T KNOW WHERE THAT SOMEWHERE IS...
BUT I DO KNOW WHERE I AM!
WAIT!
TOO BRIGHT!
AND WHERE I AM GOING!
I AM GOING TO FIND MY FRIENDS!
DON'T LEAVE YOUR FEARS!
YOU ARE POWERFUL, FEAR--

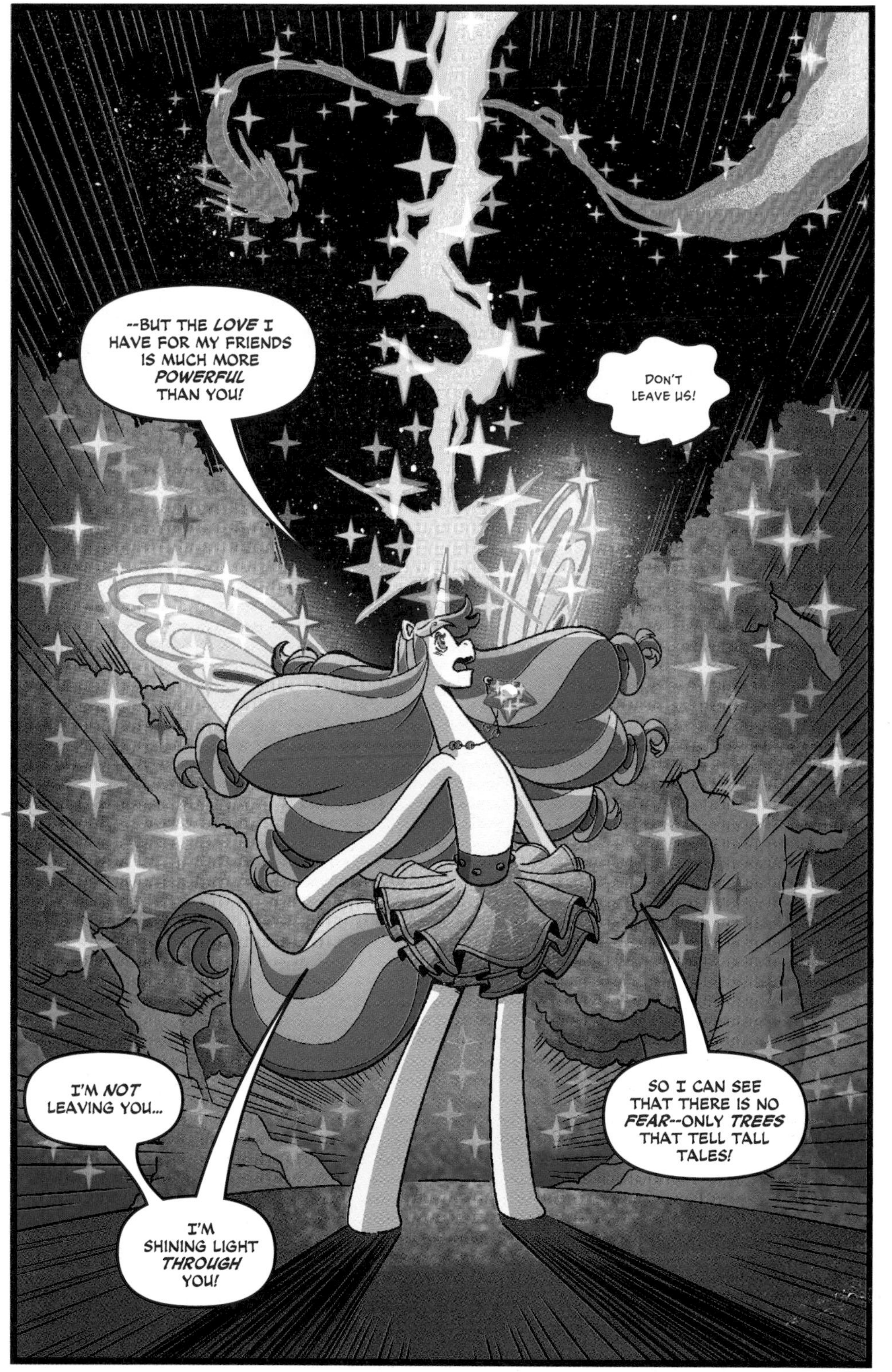
--BUT THE LOVE I HAVE FOR MY FRIENDS IS MUCH MORE POWERFUL THAN YOU!
DON'T LEAVE US!
I'M NOT LEAVING YOU...
I'M SHINING LIGHT THROUGH YOU!
SO I CAN SEE THAT THERE IS NO FEAR--ONLY TREES THAT TELL TALL TALES!

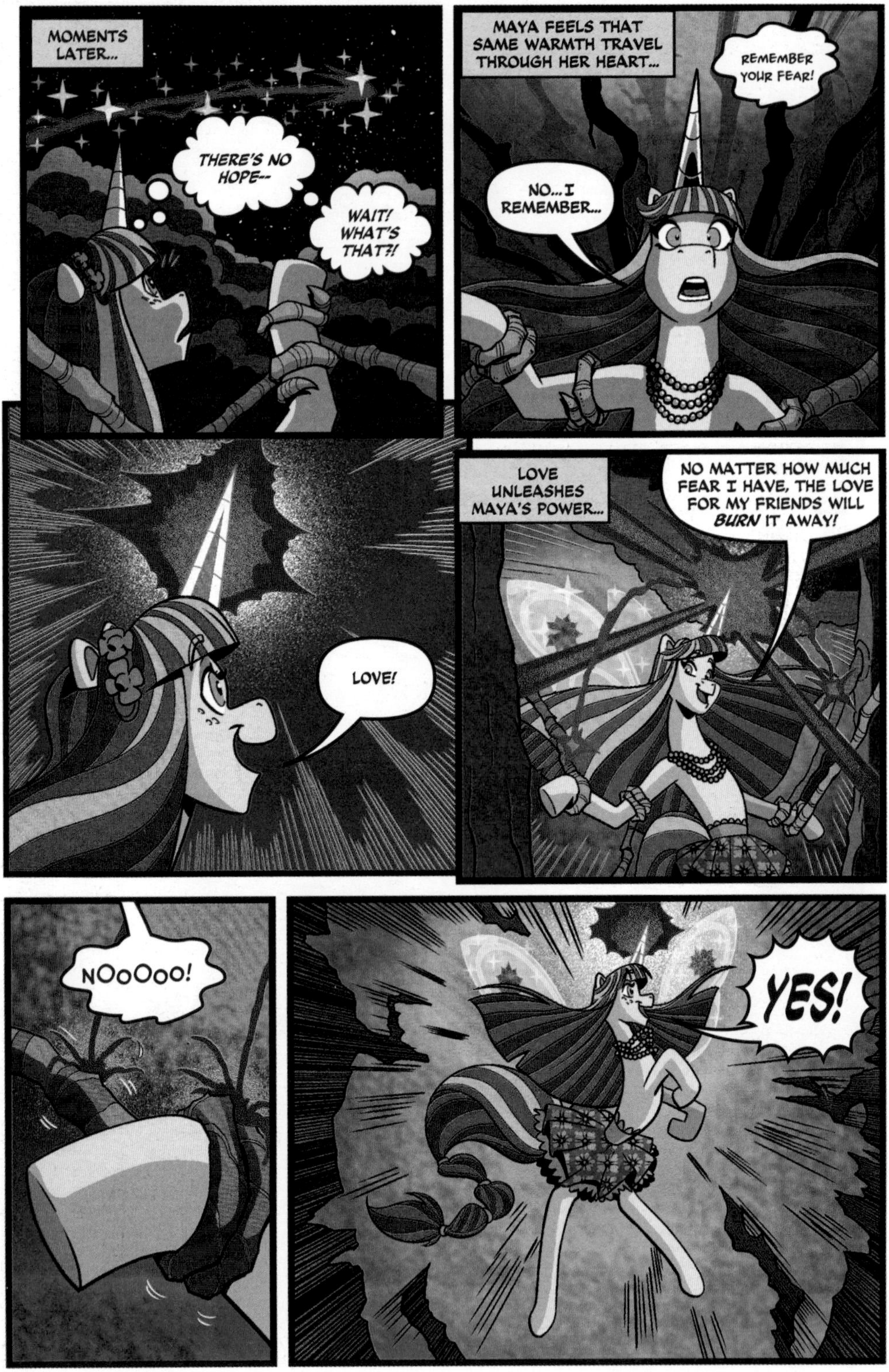

MOMENTS LATER...
THERE'S NO HOPE--
WAIT! WHAT'S THAT?!
MAYA FEELS THAT SAME WARMTH TRAVEL THROUGH HER HEART...
REMEMBER YOUR FEAR!
NO... I REMEMBER...
LOVE!
LOVE UNLEASHES MAYA'S POWER...
NO MATTER HOW MUCH FEAR I HAVE, THE LOVE FOR MY FRIENDS WILL BURN IT AWAY!
NOOOOO!
YES!

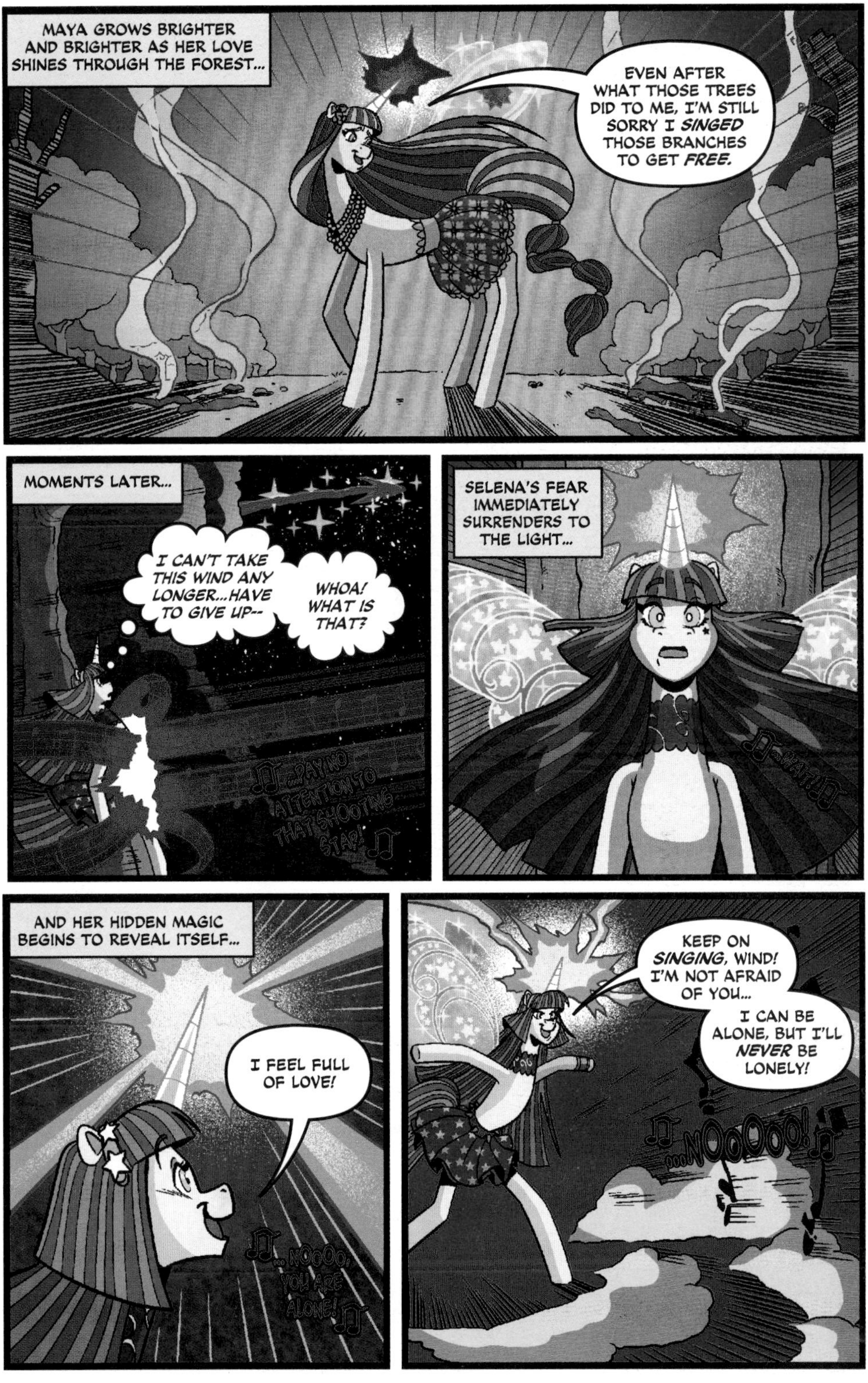
MAYA GROWS BRIGHTER AND BRIGHTER AS HER LOVE SHINES THROUGH THE FOREST...
EVEN AFTER WHAT THOSE TREES DID TO ME, I'M STILL SORRY I *SINGED* THOSE BRANCHES TO GET *FREE.*
MOMENTS LATER...
*I CAN'T TAKE THIS WIND ANY LONGER...HAVE TO GIVE UP--*
*WHOA! WHAT IS THAT?*
...PAY NO ATTENTION TO THAT SHOOTING STAR!
SELENA'S FEAR IMMEDIATELY SURRENDERS TO THE LIGHT...
...WHAT!
AND HER HIDDEN MAGIC BEGINS TO REVEAL ITSELF...
I FEEL FULL OF LOVE!
...NOOOO, YOU ARE ALONE!
KEEP ON *SINGING,* WIND! I'M NOT AFRAID OF YOU...
I CAN BE ALONE, BUT I'LL *NEVER* BE LONELY!
...NOOOOO!

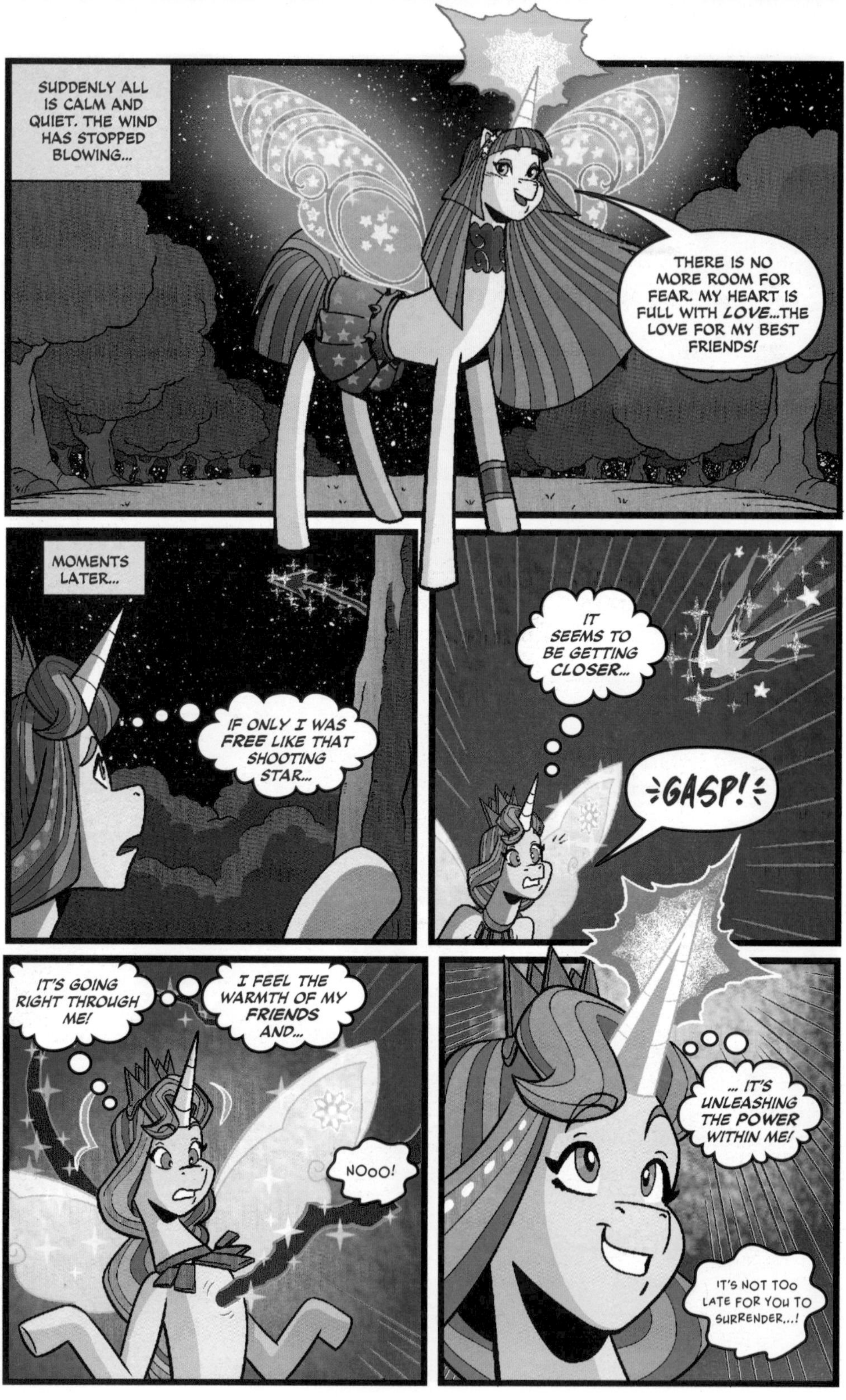
SUDDENLY ALL IS CALM AND QUIET. THE WIND HAS STOPPED BLOWING...
THERE IS NO MORE ROOM FOR FEAR. MY HEART IS FULL WITH LOVE...THE LOVE FOR MY BEST FRIENDS!
MOMENTS LATER...
IF ONLY I WAS FREE LIKE THAT SHOOTING STAR...
IT SEEMS TO BE GETTING CLOSER...
GASP!
IT'S GOING RIGHT THROUGH ME!
I FEEL THE WARMTH OF MY FRIENDS AND...
NOoO!
... IT'S UNLEASHING THE POWER WITHIN ME!
IT'S NOT TOO LATE FOR YOU TO SURRENDER...!

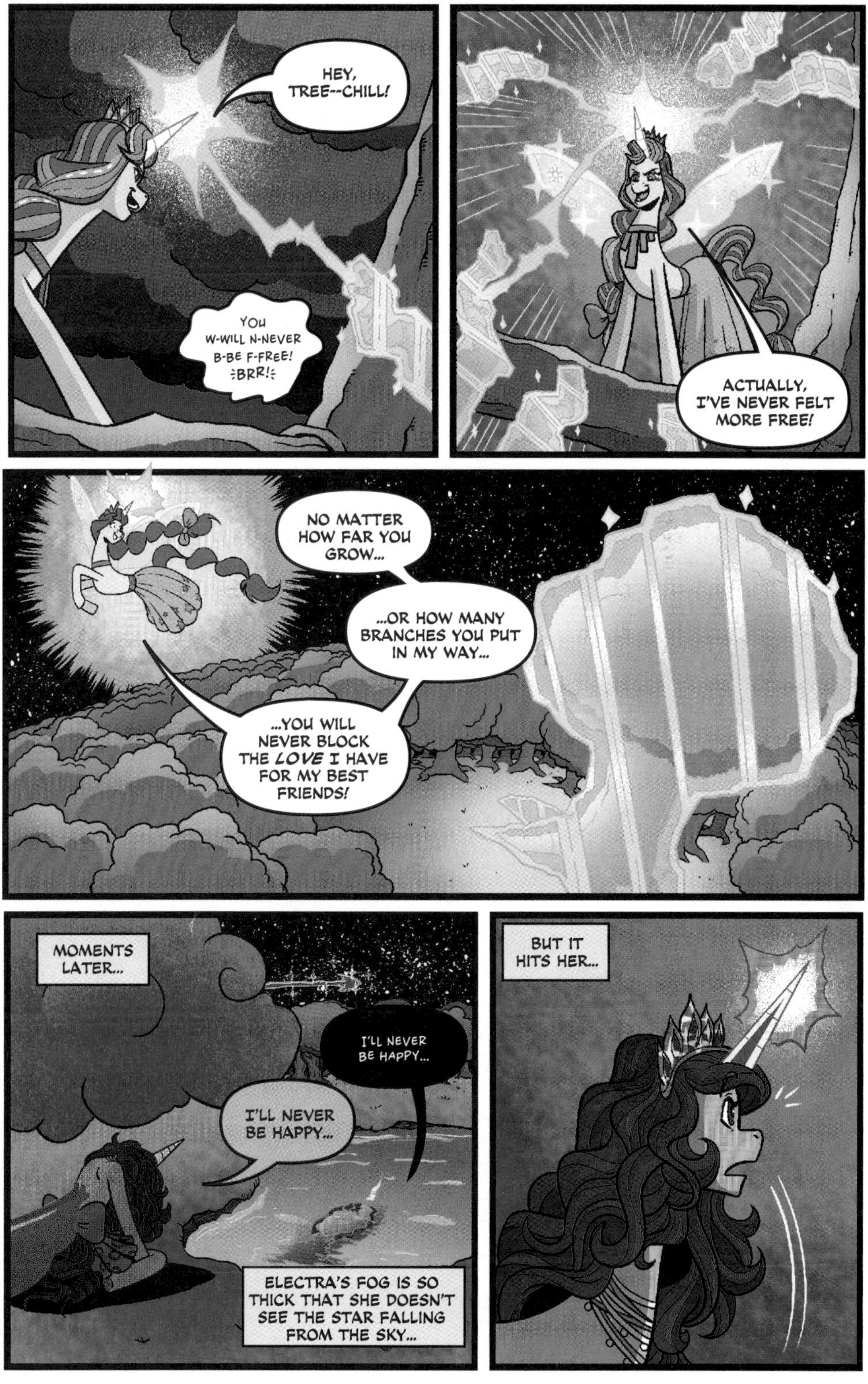
HEY, TREE--CHILL!
YOU W-WILL N-NEVER B-BE F-FREE! BRR!
ACTUALLY, I'VE NEVER FELT MORE FREE!
NO MATTER HOW FAR YOU GROW...
...OR HOW MANY BRANCHES YOU PUT IN MY WAY...
...YOU WILL NEVER BLOCK THE LOVE I HAVE FOR MY BEST FRIENDS!
MOMENTS LATER...
I'LL NEVER BE HAPPY...
I'LL NEVER BE HAPPY...
ELECTRA'S FOG IS SO THICK THAT SHE DOESN'T SEE THE STAR FALLING FROM THE SKY...
BUT IT HITS HER...

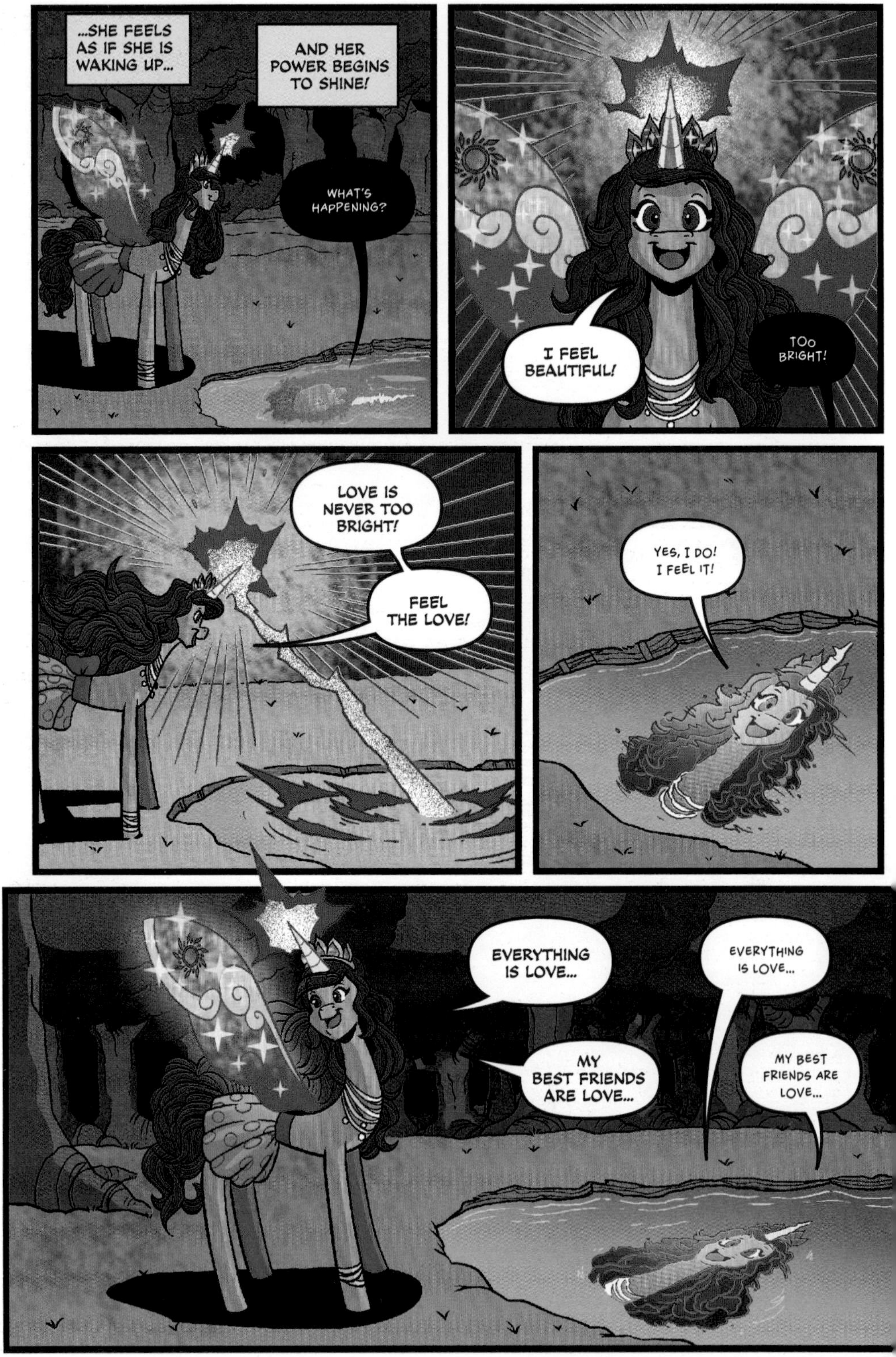
...SHE FEELS AS IF SHE IS WAKING UP...
AND HER POWER BEGINS TO SHINE!
WHAT'S HAPPENING?
I FEEL BEAUTIFUL!
TOO BRIGHT!
LOVE IS NEVER TOO BRIGHT!
FEEL THE LOVE!
YES, I DO! I FEEL IT!
EVERYTHING IS LOVE...
EVERYTHING IS LOVE...
MY BEST FRIENDS ARE LOVE...
MY BEST FRIENDS ARE LOVE...

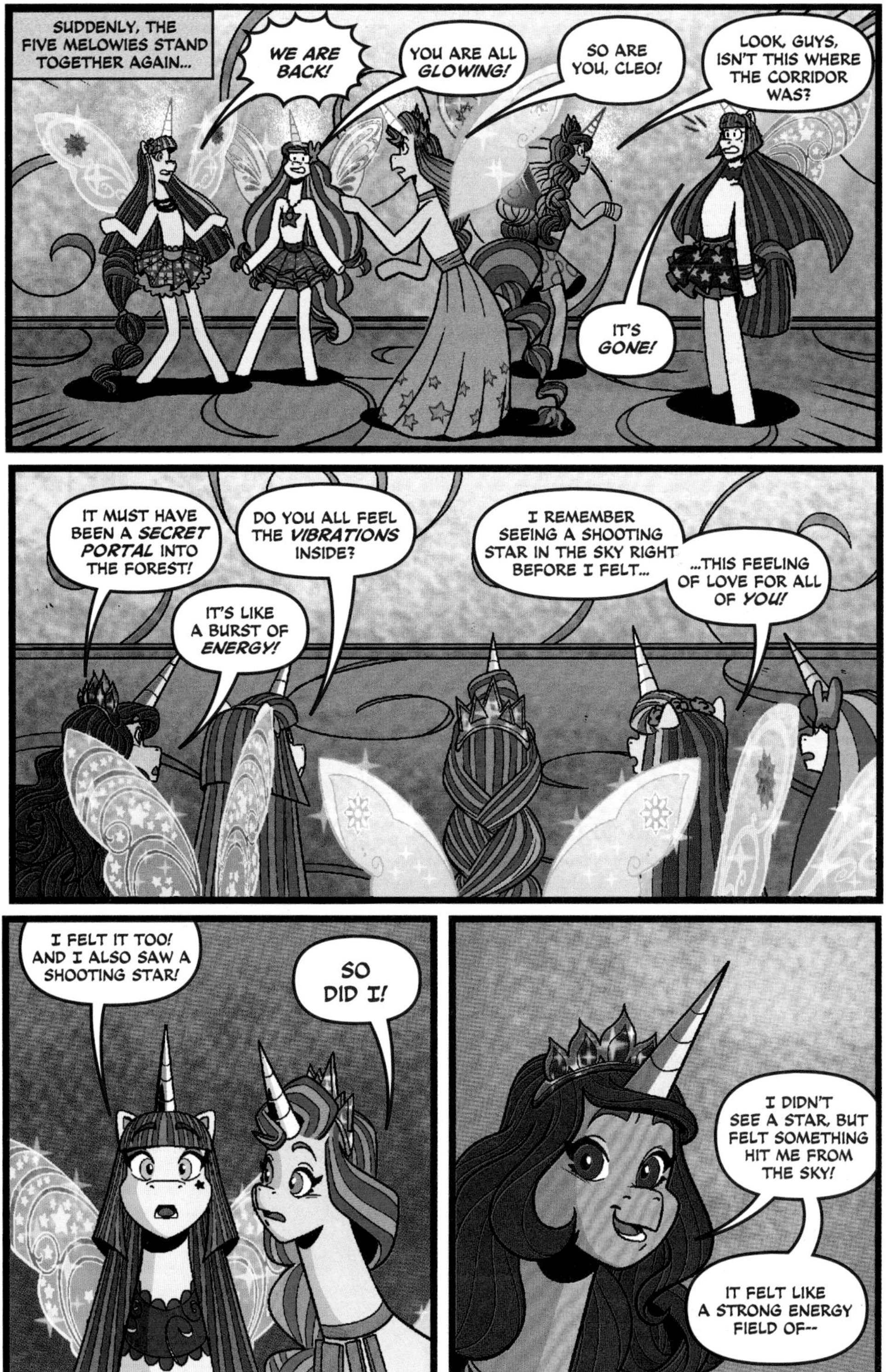
SUDDENLY, THE FIVE MELOWIES STAND TOGETHER AGAIN...
WE ARE BACK!
YOU ARE ALL GLOWING!
SO ARE YOU, CLEO!
LOOK, GUYS, ISN'T THIS WHERE THE CORRIDOR WAS?
IT'S GONE!
IT MUST HAVE BEEN A SECRET PORTAL INTO THE FOREST!
DO YOU ALL FEEL THE VIBRATIONS INSIDE?
IT'S LIKE A BURST OF ENERGY!
I REMEMBER SEEING A SHOOTING STAR IN THE SKY RIGHT BEFORE I FELT...
...THIS FEELING OF LOVE FOR ALL OF YOU!
I FELT IT TOO! AND I ALSO SAW A SHOOTING STAR!
SO DID I!
I DIDN'T SEE A STAR, BUT FELT SOMETHING HIT ME FROM THE SKY!
IT FELT LIKE A STRONG ENERGY FIELD OF--

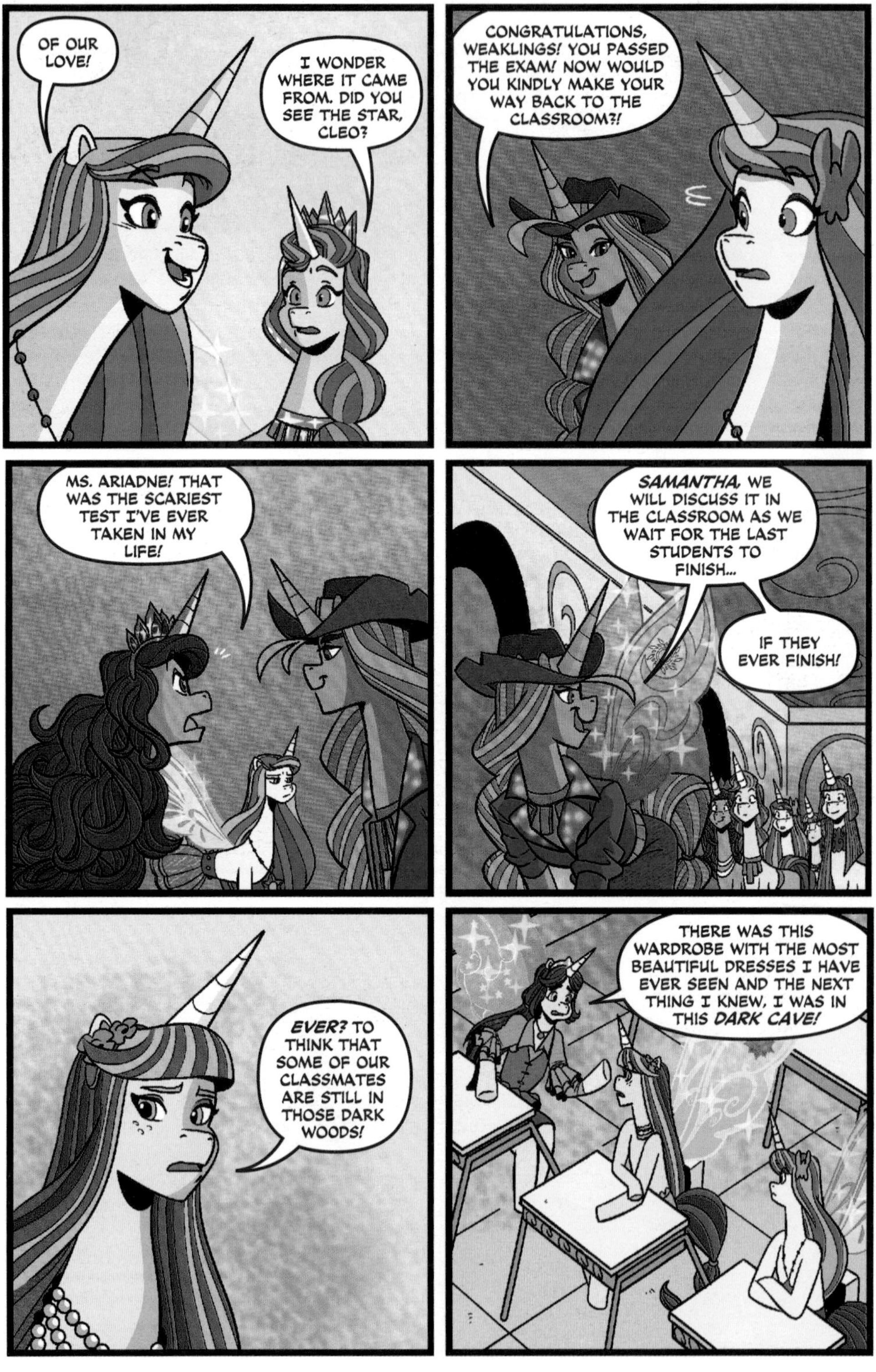

OF OUR LOVE!
I WONDER WHERE IT CAME FROM. DID YOU SEE THE STAR, CLEO?
CONGRATULATIONS, WEAKLINGS! YOU PASSED THE EXAM! NOW WOULD YOU KINDLY MAKE YOUR WAY BACK TO THE CLASSROOM?!
MS. ARIADNE! THAT WAS THE SCARIEST TEST I'VE EVER TAKEN IN MY LIFE!
SAMANTHA, WE WILL DISCUSS IT IN THE CLASSROOM AS WE WAIT FOR THE LAST STUDENTS TO FINISH...
IF THEY EVER FINISH!
EVER? TO THINK THAT SOME OF OUR CLASSMATES ARE STILL IN THOSE DARK WOODS!
THERE WAS THIS WARDROBE WITH THE MOST BEAUTIFUL DRESSES I HAVE EVER SEEN AND THE NEXT THING I KNEW, I WAS IN THIS DARK CAVE!

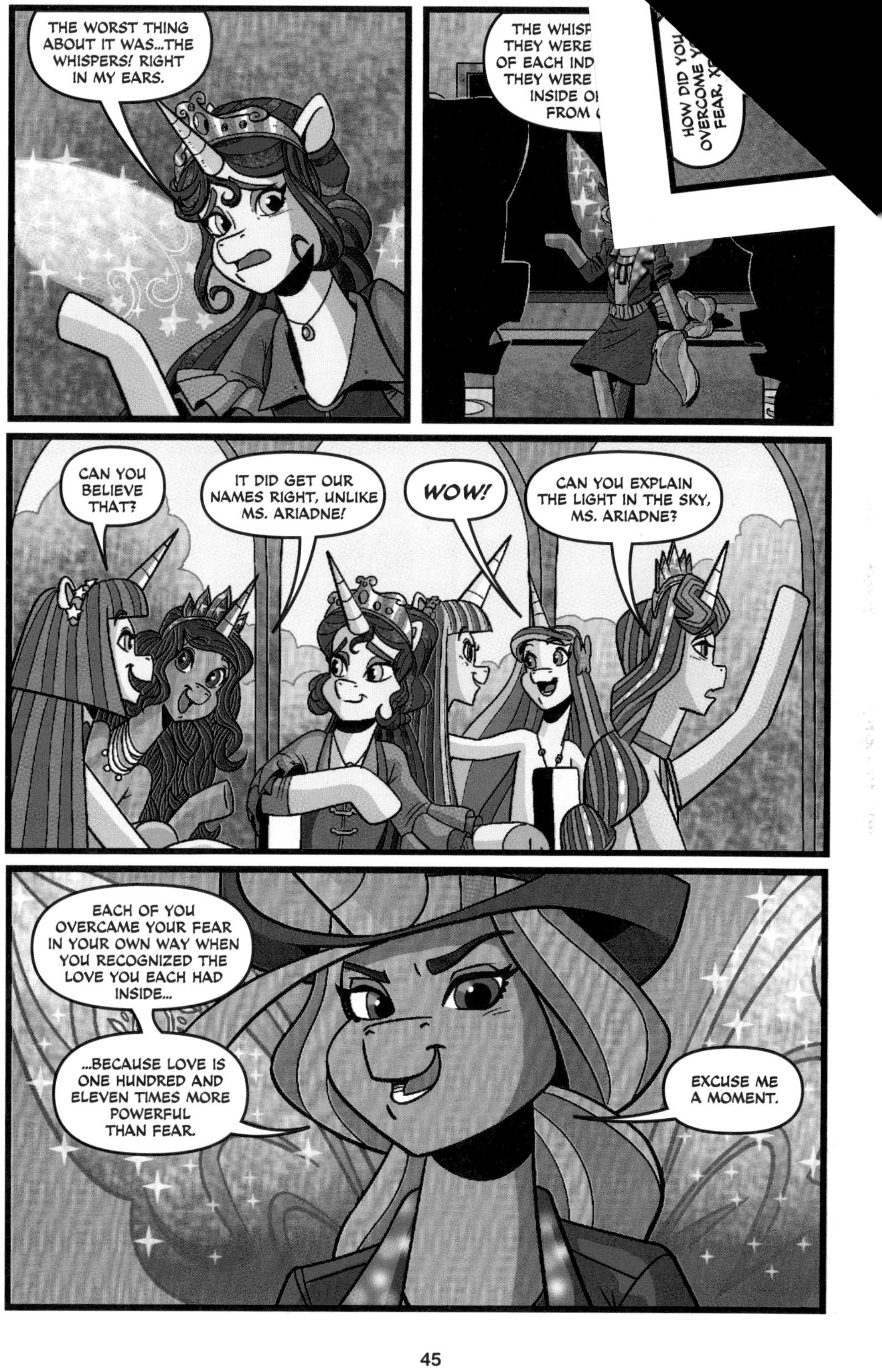
THE WORST THING ABOUT IT WAS...THE WHISPERS! RIGHT IN MY EARS.
THE WHISP THEY WERE OF EACH IND THEY WERE INSIDE OI FROM
CAN YOU BELIEVE THAT?
IT DID GET OUR NAMES RIGHT, UNLIKE MS. ARIADNE!
WOW!
CAN YOU EXPLAIN THE LIGHT IN THE SKY, MS. ARIADNE?
EACH OF YOU OVERCAME YOUR FEAR IN YOUR OWN WAY WHEN YOU RECOGNIZED THE LOVE YOU EACH HAD INSIDE...
...BECAUSE LOVE IS ONE HUNDRED AND ELEVEN TIMES MORE POWERFUL THAN FEAR.
EXCUSE ME A MOMENT.

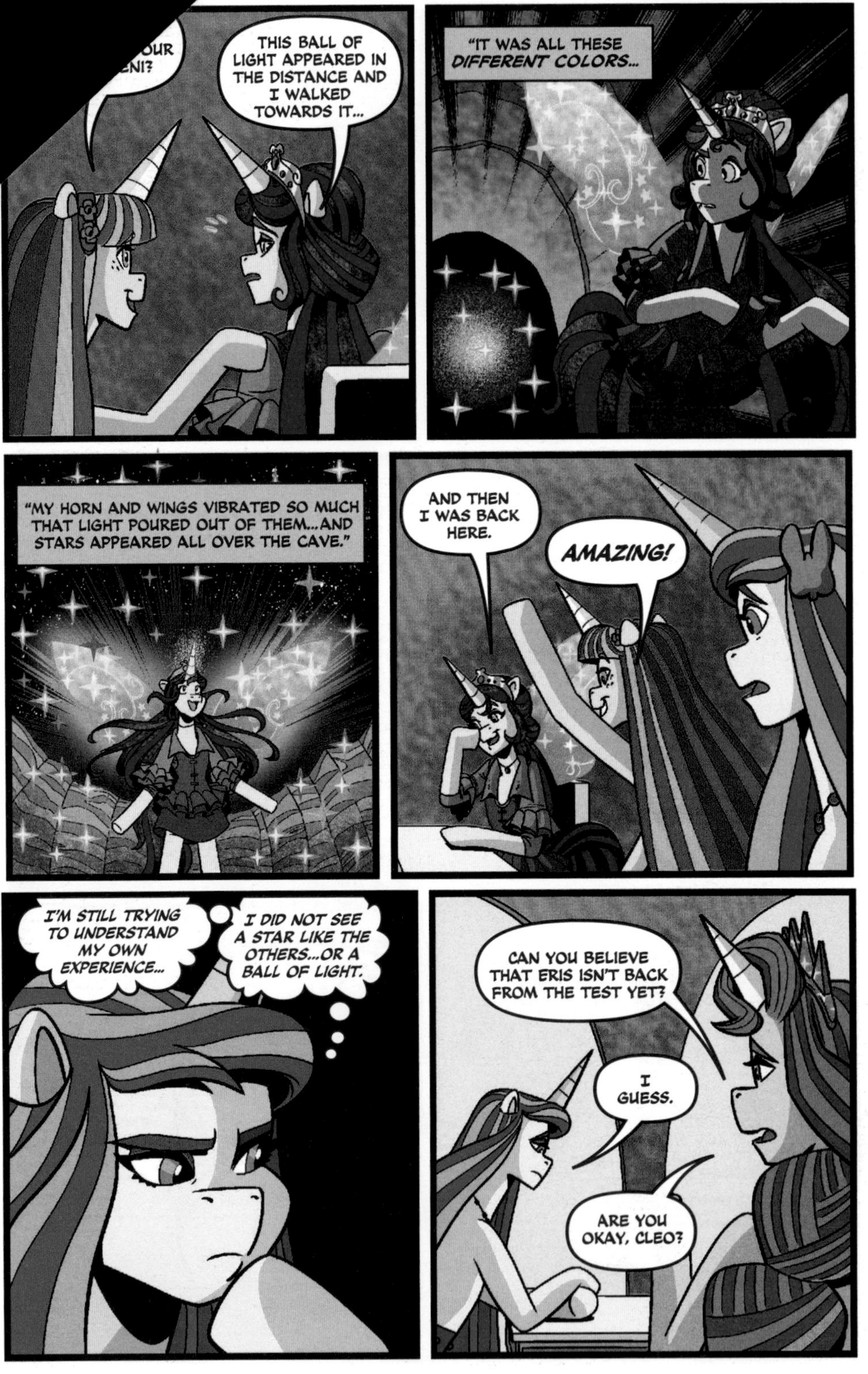
THIS BALL OF LIGHT APPEARED IN THE DISTANCE AND I WALKED TOWARDS IT...
"IT WAS ALL THESE DIFFERENT COLORS...
"MY HORN AND WINGS VIBRATED SO MUCH THAT LIGHT POURED OUT OF THEM...AND STARS APPEARED ALL OVER THE CAVE."
AND THEN I WAS BACK HERE.
AMAZING!
I'M STILL TRYING TO UNDERSTAND MY OWN EXPERIENCE...
I DID NOT SEE A STAR LIKE THE OTHERS...OR A BALL OF LIGHT.
CAN YOU BELIEVE THAT ERIS ISN'T BACK FROM THE TEST YET?
I GUESS.
ARE YOU OKAY, CLEO?

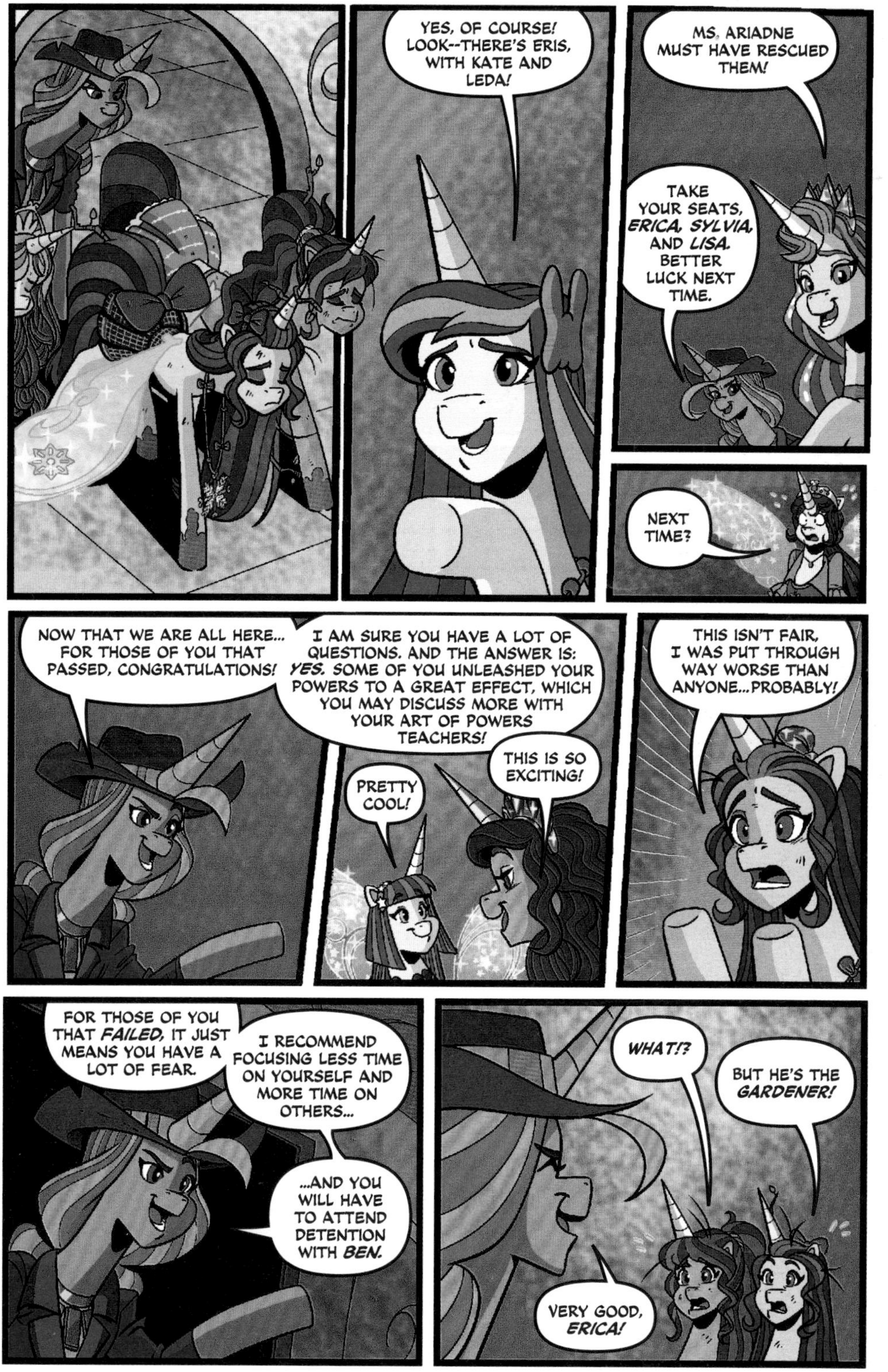
YES, OF COURSE! LOOK--THERE'S ERIS, WITH KATE AND LEDA!
MS. ARIADNE MUST HAVE RESCUED THEM!
TAKE YOUR SEATS, ERICA, SYLVIA, AND LISA. BETTER LUCK NEXT TIME.
NEXT TIME?
NOW THAT WE ARE ALL HERE... FOR THOSE OF YOU THAT PASSED, CONGRATULATIONS!
I AM SURE YOU HAVE A LOT OF QUESTIONS. AND THE ANSWER IS: YES. SOME OF YOU UNLEASHED YOUR POWERS TO A GREAT EFFECT, WHICH YOU MAY DISCUSS MORE WITH YOUR ART OF POWERS TEACHERS!
PRETTY COOL!
THIS IS SO EXCITING!
THIS ISN'T FAIR, I WAS PUT THROUGH WAY WORSE THAN ANYONE...PROBABLY!
FOR THOSE OF YOU THAT FAILED, IT JUST MEANS YOU HAVE A LOT OF FEAR.
I RECOMMEND FOCUSING LESS TIME ON YOURSELF AND MORE TIME ON OTHERS...
...AND YOU WILL HAVE TO ATTEND DETENTION WITH BEN.
WHAT!?
BUT HE'S THE GARDENER!
VERY GOOD, ERICA!

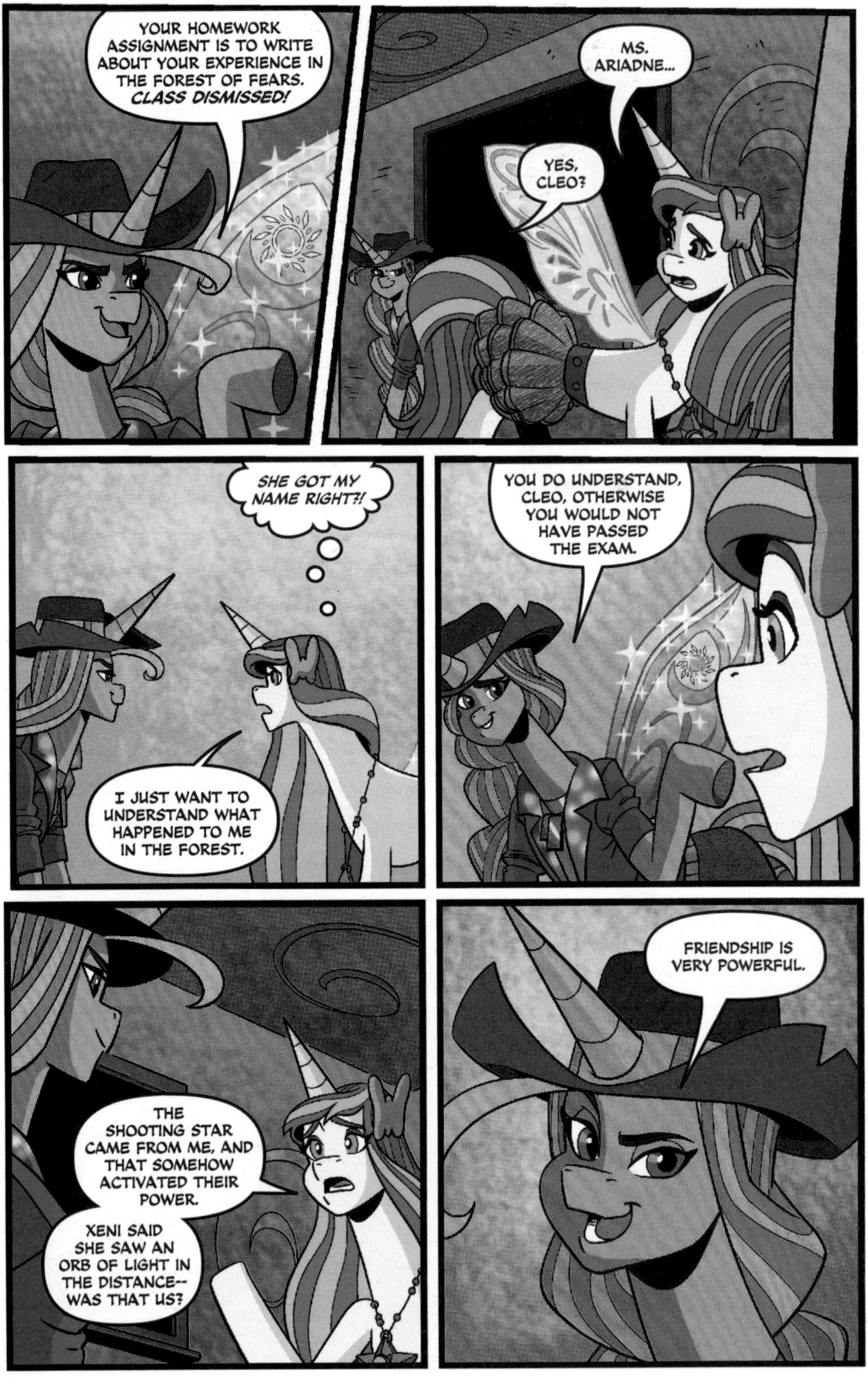
YOUR HOMEWORK ASSIGNMENT IS TO WRITE ABOUT YOUR EXPERIENCE IN THE FOREST OF FEARS. *CLASS DISMISSED!*
MS. ARIADNE...
YES, CLEO?
*SHE GOT MY NAME RIGHT?!*
I JUST WANT TO UNDERSTAND WHAT HAPPENED TO ME IN THE FOREST.
YOU DO UNDERSTAND, CLEO, OTHERWISE YOU WOULD NOT HAVE PASSED THE EXAM.
THE SHOOTING STAR CAME FROM ME, AND THAT SOMEHOW ACTIVATED THEIR POWER.
XENI SAID SHE SAW AN ORB OF LIGHT IN THE DISTANCE-- WAS THAT US?
FRIENDSHIP IS VERY POWERFUL.

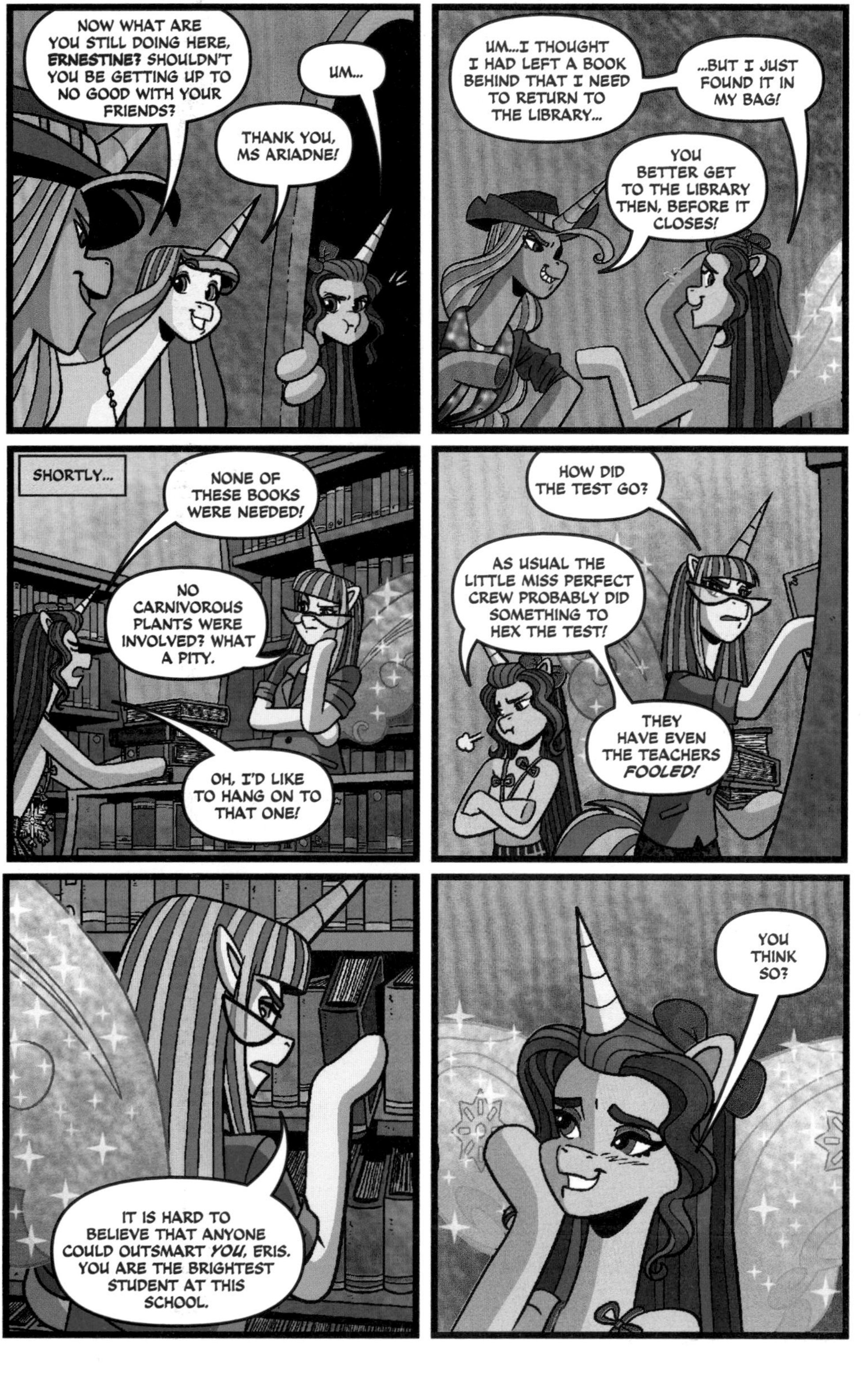
NOW WHAT ARE YOU STILL DOING HERE, ERNESTINE? SHOULDN'T YOU BE GETTING UP TO NO GOOD WITH YOUR FRIENDS?
UM...
THANK YOU, MS ARIADNE!
UM...I THOUGHT I HAD LEFT A BOOK BEHIND THAT I NEED TO RETURN TO THE LIBRARY...
...BUT I JUST FOUND IT IN MY BAG!
YOU BETTER GET TO THE LIBRARY THEN, BEFORE IT CLOSES!
SHORTLY...
NONE OF THESE BOOKS WERE NEEDED!
NO CARNIVOROUS PLANTS WERE INVOLVED? WHAT A PITY.
OH, I'D LIKE TO HANG ON TO THAT ONE!
HOW DID THE TEST GO?
AS USUAL THE LITTLE MISS PERFECT CREW PROBABLY DID SOMETHING TO HEX THE TEST!
THEY HAVE EVEN THE TEACHERS FOOLED!
IT IS HARD TO BELIEVE THAT ANYONE COULD OUTSMART YOU, ERIS. YOU ARE THE BRIGHTEST STUDENT AT THIS SCHOOL.
YOU THINK SO?

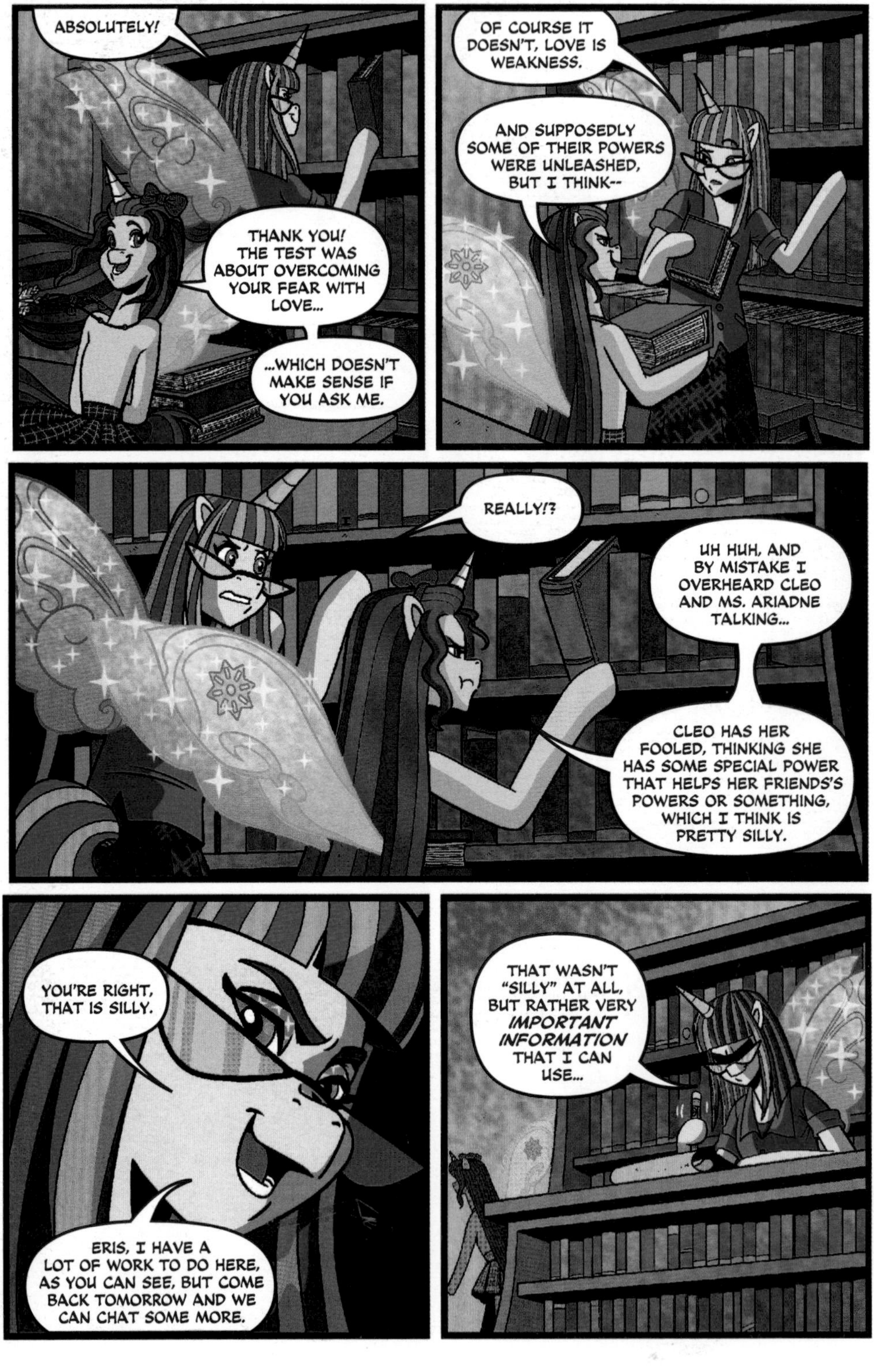
ABSOLUTELY!
THANK YOU! THE TEST WAS ABOUT OVERCOMING YOUR FEAR WITH LOVE...
...WHICH DOESN'T MAKE SENSE IF YOU ASK ME.
OF COURSE IT DOESN'T, LOVE IS WEAKNESS.
AND SUPPOSEDLY SOME OF THEIR POWERS WERE UNLEASHED, BUT I THINK--
REALLY!?
UH HUH, AND BY MISTAKE I OVERHEARD CLEO AND MS. ARIADNE TALKING...
CLEO HAS HER FOOLED, THINKING SHE HAS SOME SPECIAL POWER THAT HELPS HER FRIENDS'S POWERS OR SOMETHING, WHICH I THINK IS PRETTY SILLY.
YOU'RE RIGHT, THAT IS SILLY.
ERIS, I HAVE A LOT OF WORK TO DO HERE, AS YOU CAN SEE, BUT COME BACK TOMORROW AND WE CAN CHAT SOME MORE.
THAT WASN'T "SILLY" AT ALL, BUT RATHER VERY *IMPORTANT INFORMATION* THAT I CAN USE...

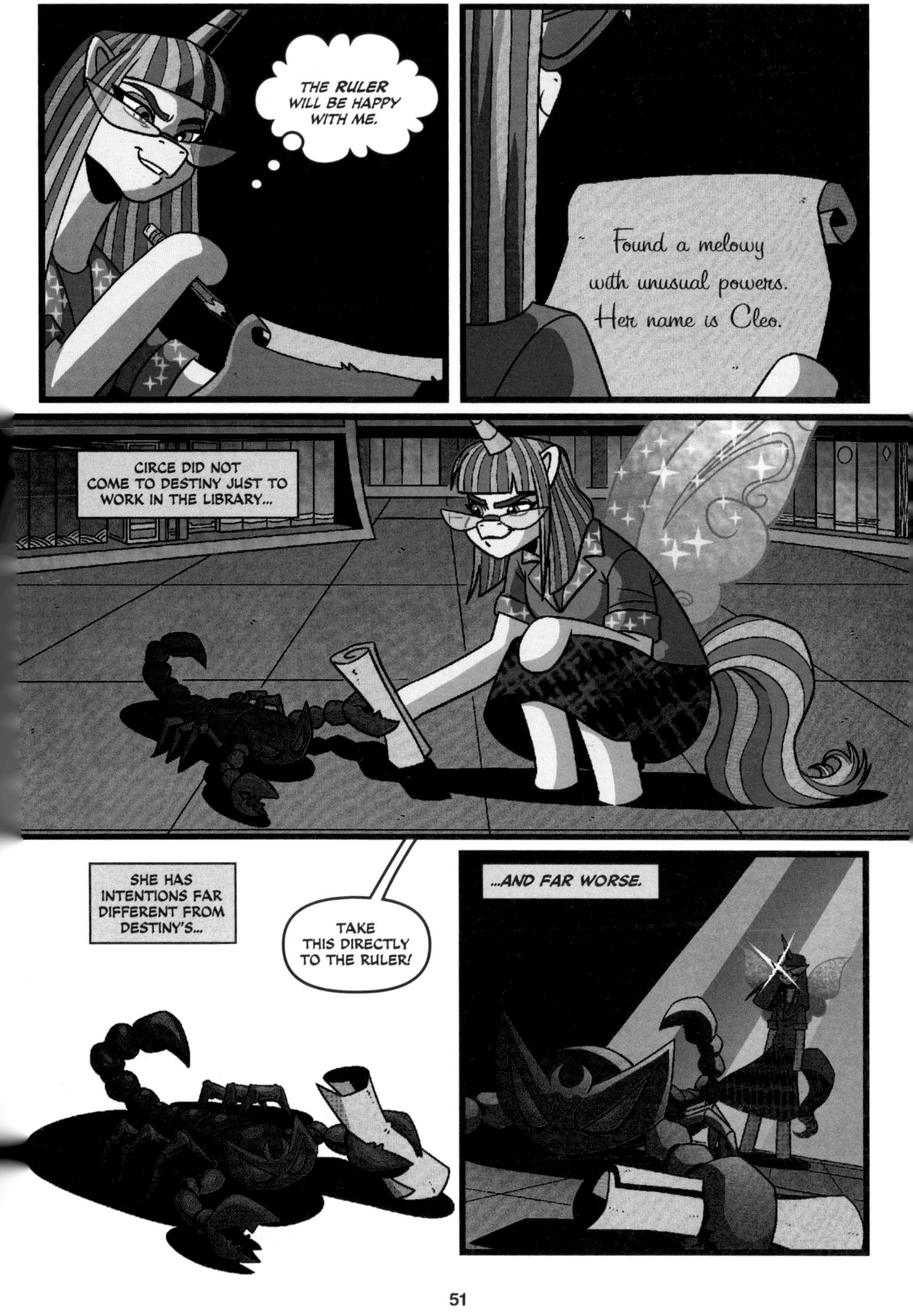
THE RULER WILL BE HAPPY WITH ME.
Found a melowy with unusual powers. Her name is Cleo.
CIRCE DID NOT COME TO DESTINY JUST TO WORK IN THE LIBRARY...
SHE HAS INTENTIONS FAR DIFFERENT FROM DESTINY'S...
TAKE THIS DIRECTLY TO THE RULER!
...AND FAR WORSE.

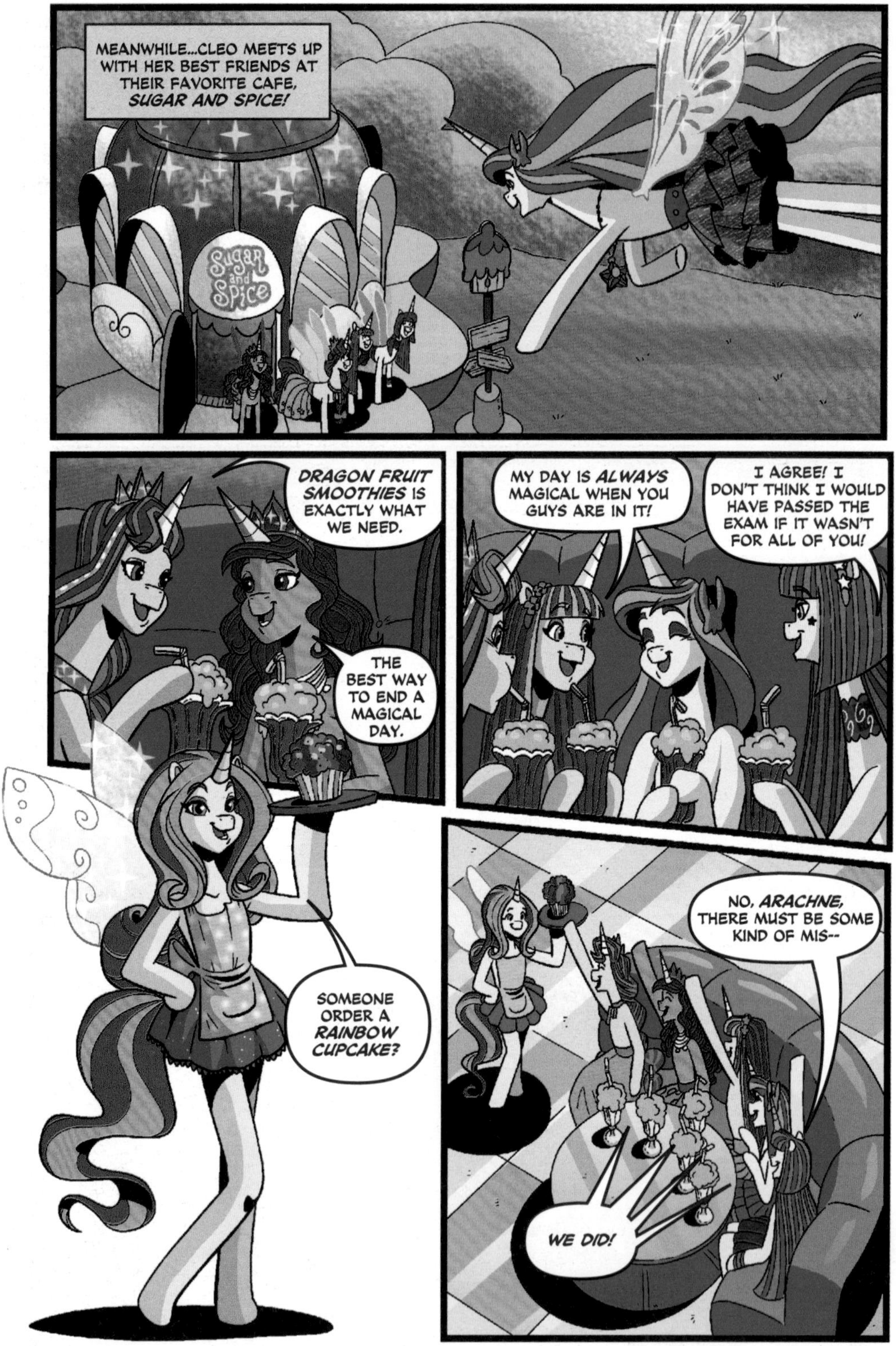
MEANWHILE...CLEO MEETS UP WITH HER BEST FRIENDS AT THEIR FAVORITE CAFE, *SUGAR AND SPICE!*
Sugar and Spice
*DRAGON FRUIT SMOOTHIES* IS EXACTLY WHAT WE NEED.
THE BEST WAY TO END A MAGICAL DAY.
MY DAY IS *ALWAYS* MAGICAL WHEN YOU GUYS ARE IN IT!
I AGREE! I DON'T THINK I WOULD HAVE PASSED THE EXAM IF IT WASN'T FOR ALL OF YOU!
SOMEONE ORDER A *RAINBOW CUPCAKE?*
NO, *ARACHNE,* THERE MUST BE SOME KIND OF MIS--
*WE DID!*

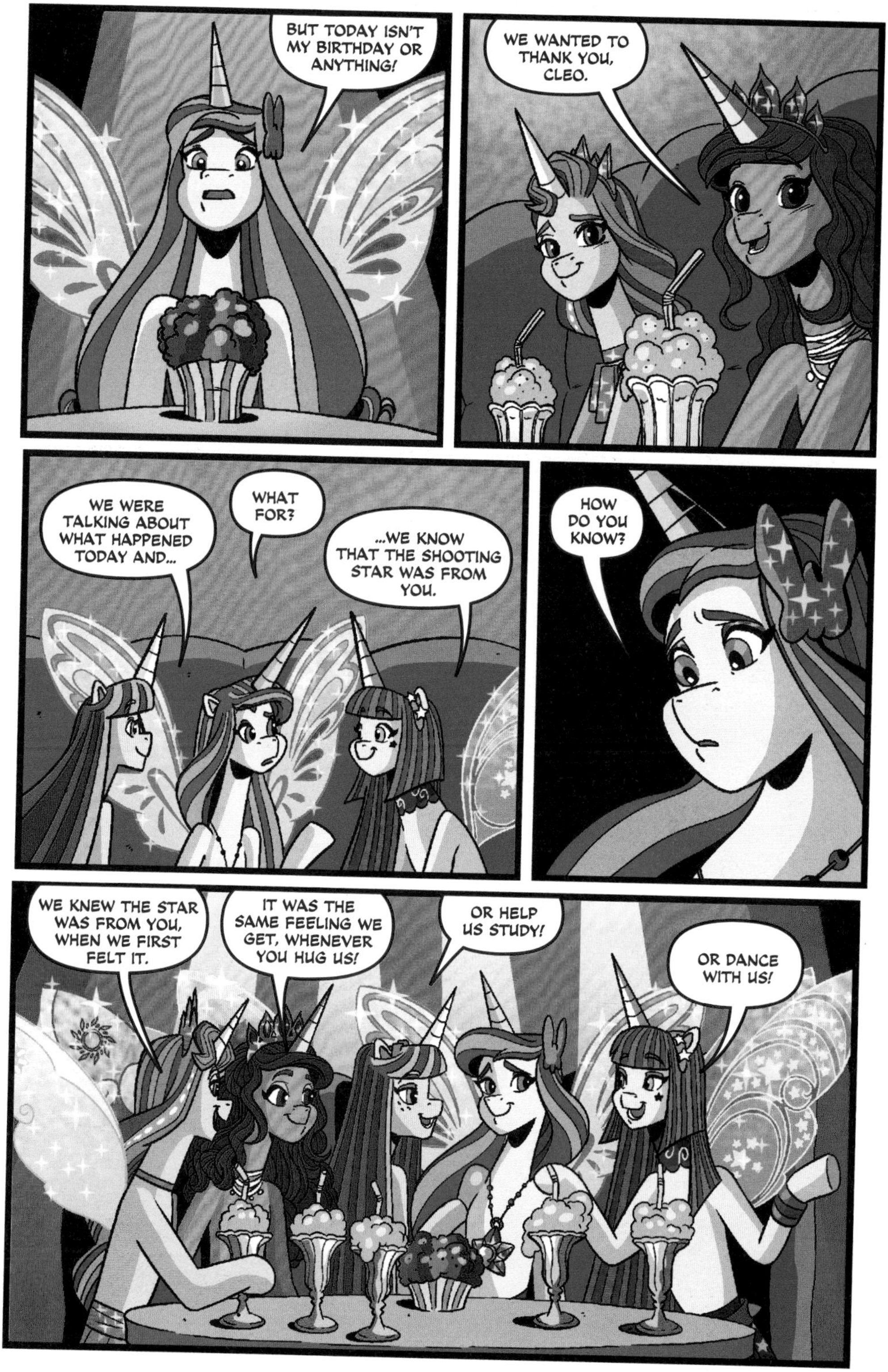

BUT TODAY ISN'T MY BIRTHDAY OR ANYTHING!
WE WANTED TO THANK YOU, CLEO.
WE WERE TALKING ABOUT WHAT HAPPENED TODAY AND...
WHAT FOR?
...WE KNOW THAT THE SHOOTING STAR WAS FROM YOU.
HOW DO YOU KNOW?
WE KNEW THE STAR WAS FROM YOU, WHEN WE FIRST FELT IT.
IT WAS THE SAME FEELING WE GET, WHENEVER YOU HUG US!
OR HELP US STUDY!
OR DANCE WITH US!

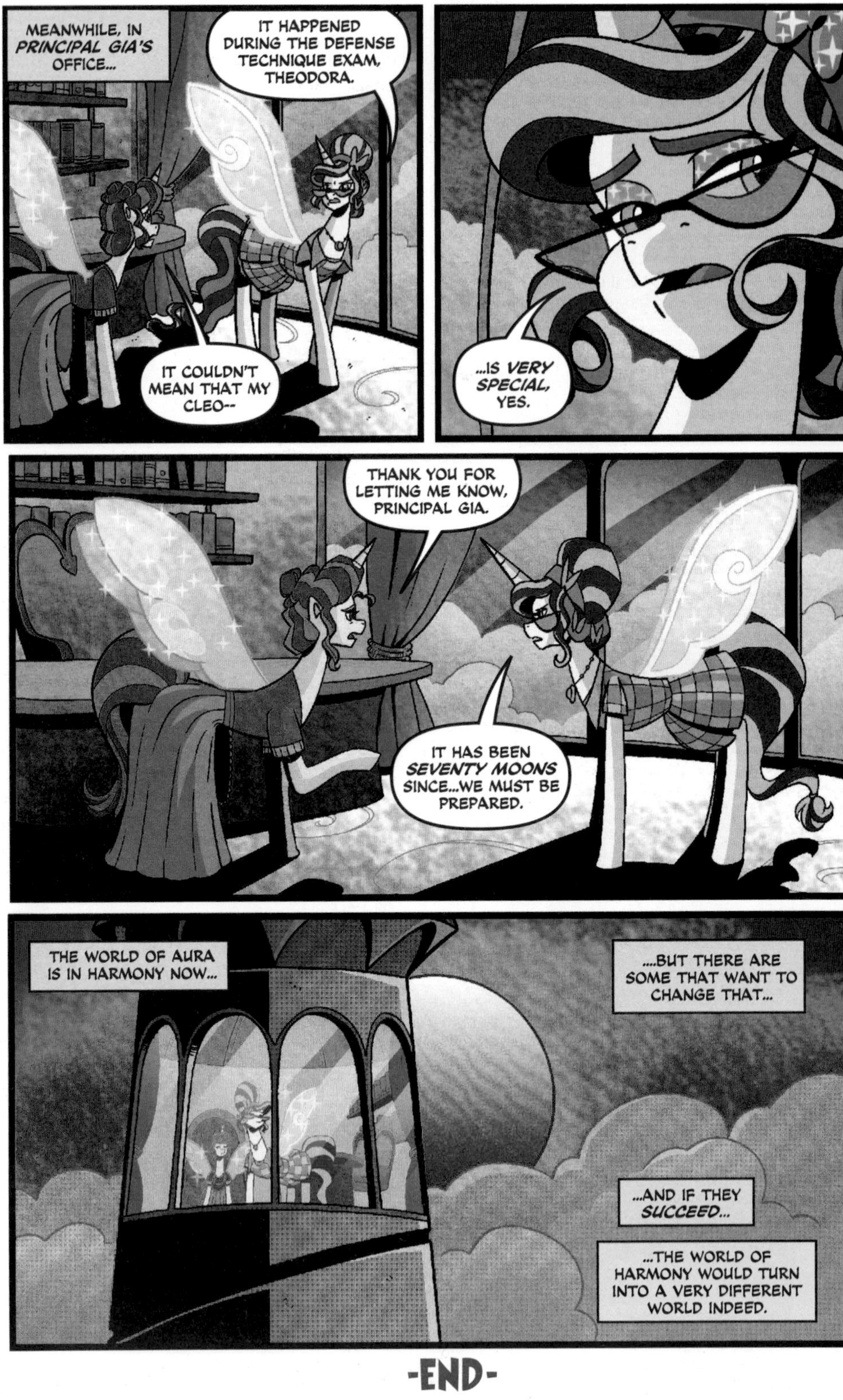
MEANWHILE, IN PRINCIPAL GIA'S OFFICE...
IT HAPPENED DURING THE DEFENSE TECHNIQUE EXAM, THEODORA.
IT COULDN'T MEAN THAT MY CLEO--
...IS VERY SPECIAL, YES.
THANK YOU FOR LETTING ME KNOW, PRINCIPAL GIA.
IT HAS BEEN SEVENTY MOONS SINCE...WE MUST BE PREPARED.
THE WORLD OF AURA IS IN HARMONY NOW...
...BUT THERE ARE SOME THAT WANT TO CHANGE THAT...
...AND IF THEY SUCCEED...
...THE WORLD OF HARMONY WOULD TURN INTO A VERY DIFFERENT WORLD INDEED.

-END-

# WATCH OUT FOR PAPERCUTZ

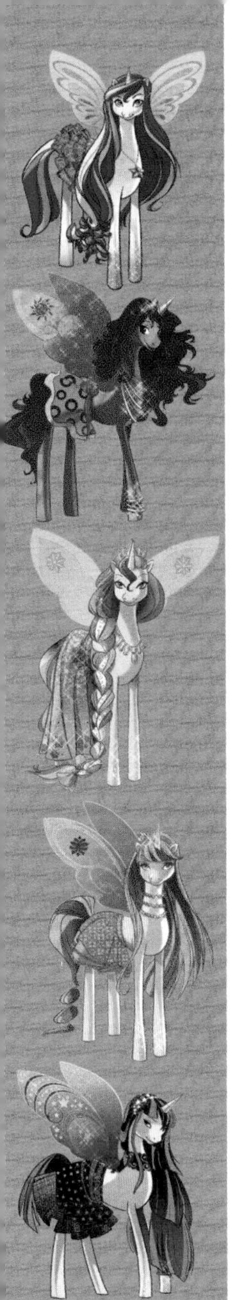

Welcome to the marvelous and magical premiere MELOWY graphic novel, by Cortney Powell and Ryan Jampole based on the characters created by Danielle Star, from Papercutz, the Pegasus-friendly folks dedicated to publishing graphic novels for all ages. I'm Jim Salicrup, the Editor-in-Chief and part-time hall monitor at Destiny. Generally, within this column, I'll take you behind-the-scenes at Papercutz and let you know what we're cooking up for you next. But before we get to that, let's talk about MELOWY a bit...

People often ask us at Papercutz how do we decide what we're going to publish? Good question! The obvious and most honest answer would be we try to find great characters, in well-written stories, illustrated with beautiful artwork, and we hope it will attract as large an audience as possible. After all, the reality of the publishing business is if you don't sell enough books, then you'll go out of business. We're entering our thirteenth year of publishing graphic novels, so we must be doing something right.

But that doesn't answer the question of why we're now launching MELOWY. The answer may surprise you, because it all started (as a great man once said) with a mouse. Back in 2008, Papercutz started publishing the graphic novel adventures of GERONIMO STILTON. He's the editor of The Rodent's Gazette, the most *famouse* newspaper on Mouse Island. Geronimo is often attempting to thwart his arch foes, The Pirate Cats, who have discovered a way to travel back in time and change history. In other words, GERONIMO STILTON is all about saving the future by protecting the past.

The GERONIMO STILTON graphic novels were so popular that we're still publishing them today, and over the years we even published the spin-off series, THEA STILTON, which featured five Mouseford Academy students who were inspired by Geronimo's sister, Thea Stilton, the famous journalist, to become journalists themselves. They even call themselves The Thea Sisters. Both GERONIMO STILTON and THEA STILTON were originally based on an original idea by Elisabetta Dami, and marketed around the world by a company called Atlantyca. We absolutely love working with everyone at Atlantyca, and when they told us about a new project that featured flying unicorns attending a magical school, we knew we had to publish MELOWY graphic novels too!

So here we are, the first MELOWY graphic novel is completed and we couldn't be more excited! We really want to know what you think of Cleo, Electra, Eris, Flora, Selena, and everyone else attending Destiny! See the box below to see how you may contact us to share your thoughts on MELOWY...

Hey, remember we said "it all started with a mouse"? Well, what better way to end this graphic novel than to offer a peek at that mouse's latest offering from Papercutz—GERONIMO STILTON 3 IN 1! It's a special book that features the first three GERONIMO STILTON graphic novels all in just one book! So let's go back to the future and enjoy the opening pages of Geronimo's very first graphic novel, "The Discovery of America." It starts on the very next page!

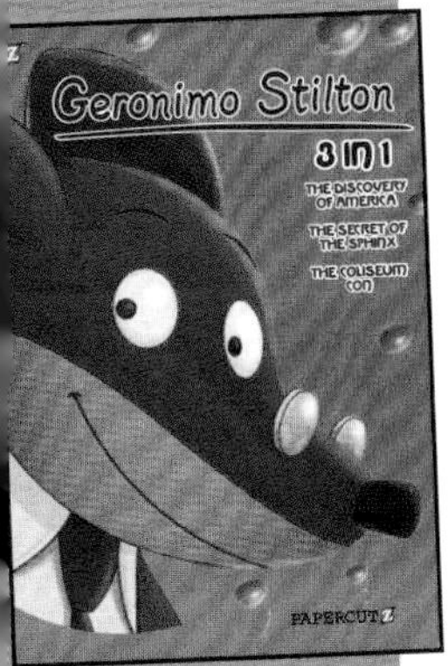
Geronimo Stilton
3 IN 1
THE DISCOVERY OF AMERICA
THE SECRET OF THE SPHINX
THE COLISEUM CON
PAPERCUTZ

If all goes well, we'll be back with MELOWY #2 "The Fashion Club of Colors" before you know it! Until then, be sure to visit papercutz.com for the latest news on MELOWY and all our other great graphic novels. And be sure to tell your friends about MELOWY too! Some things are just too wonderful to keep all to yourself!

Thanks, JIM

**STAY IN TOUCH!**

| | | | |
|---|---|---|---|
| EMAIL: | salicrup@papercutz.com | INSTAGRAM: | @papercutzgn |
| WEB: | papercutz.com | FACEBOOK: | PAPERCUTZGRAPHICNOVELS |
| TWITTER: | @papercutzgn | SNAIL MAIL: | Papercutz, 160 Broadway, Suite 700, East Wing, New York, NY 10038 |

# Here's a special preview of GERONIMO STILTON 3 IN 1 #1...

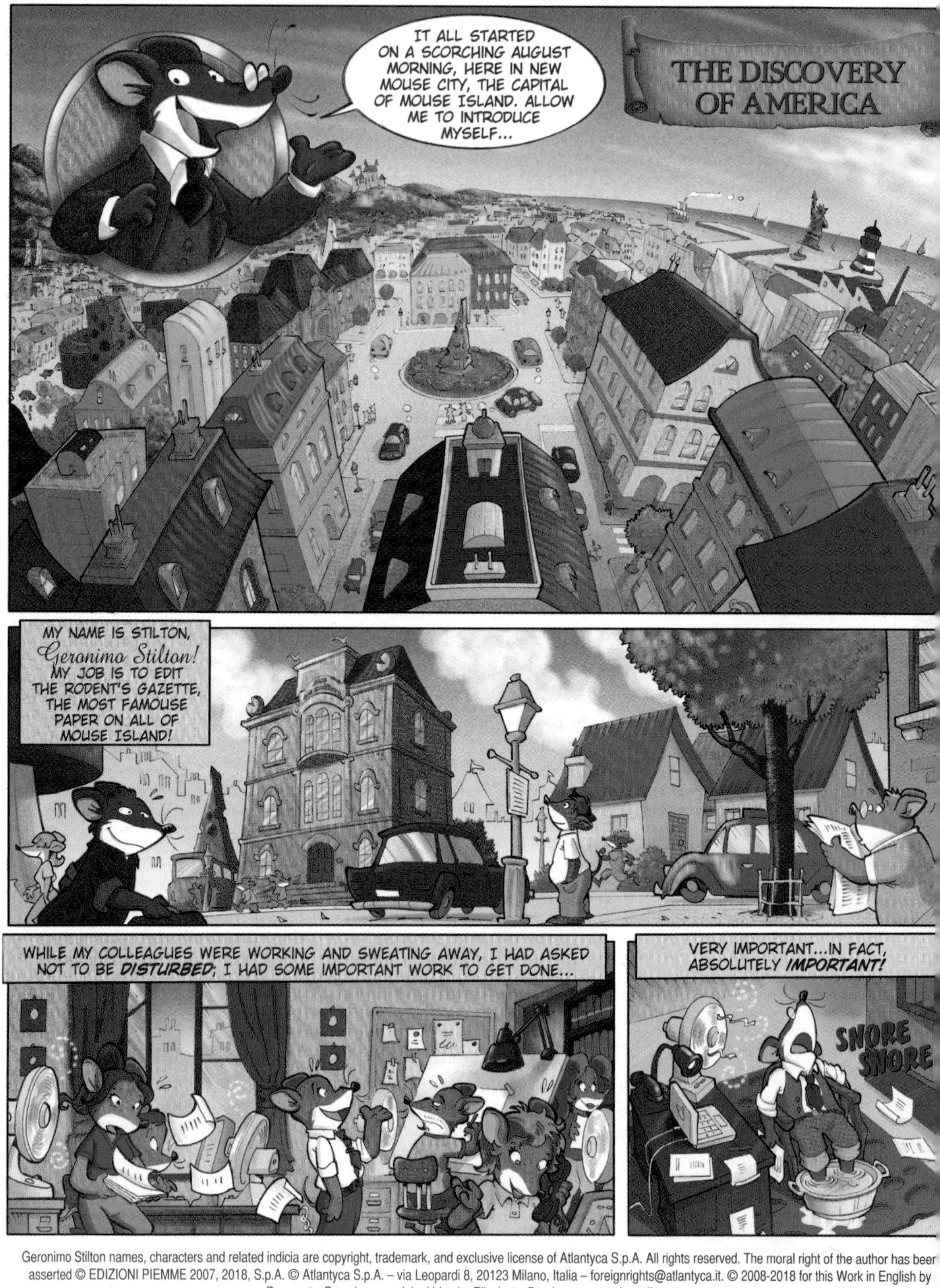

THE DISCOVERY OF AMERICA
IT ALL STARTED ON A SCORCHING AUGUST MORNING, HERE IN NEW MOUSE CITY, THE CAPITAL OF MOUSE ISLAND. ALLOW ME TO INTRODUCE MYSELF...
MY NAME IS STILTON, *Geronimo Stilton!* MY JOB IS TO EDIT THE RODENT'S GAZETTE, THE MOST FAMOUSE PAPER ON ALL OF MOUSE ISLAND!
WHILE MY COLLEAGUES WERE WORKING AND SWEATING AWAY, I HAD ASKED NOT TO BE *DISTURBED*; I HAD SOME IMPORTANT WORK TO GET DONE...
VERY IMPORTANT...IN FACT, ABSOLUTELY *IMPORTANT!*
SNORE SNORE

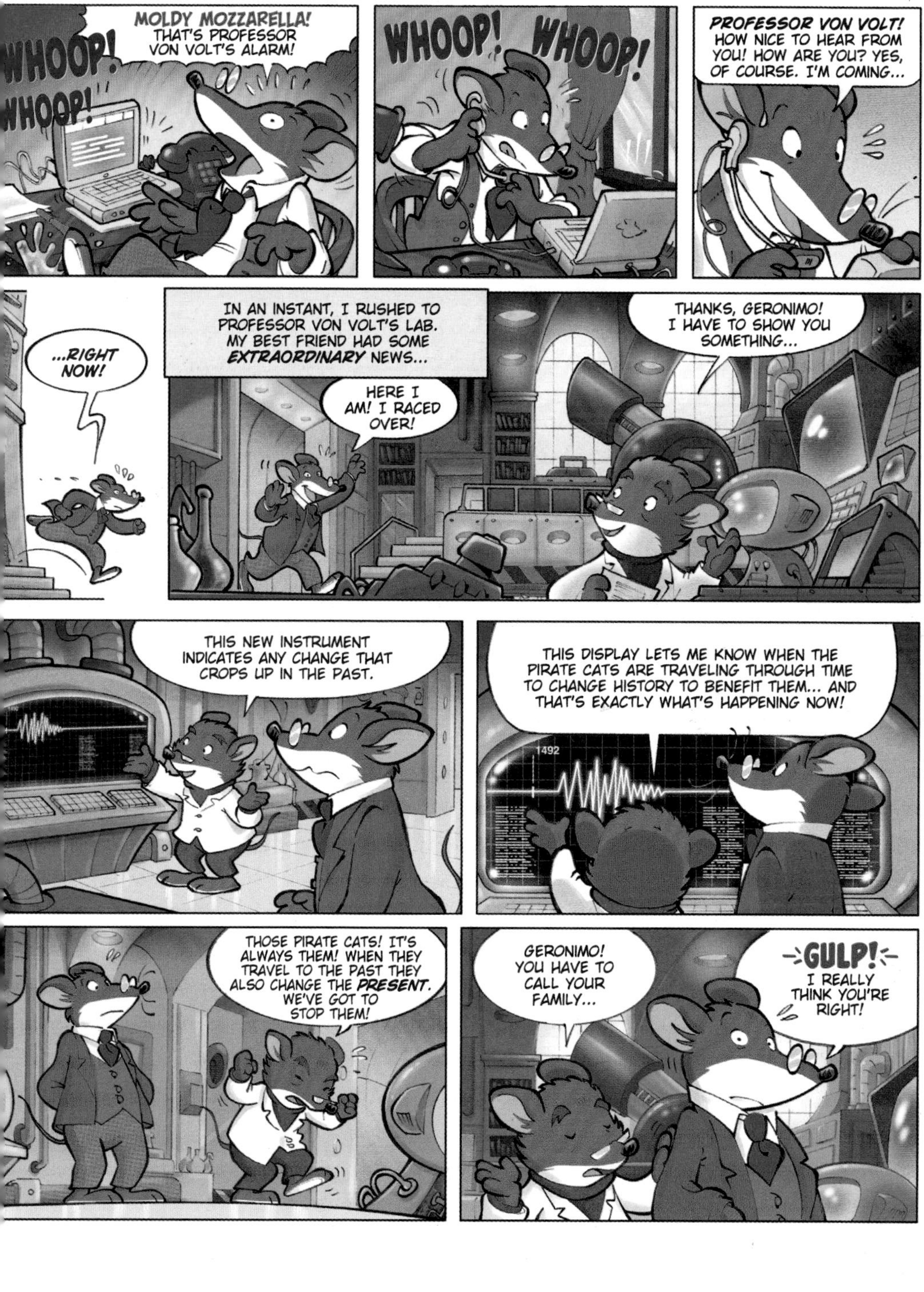
MOLDY MOZZARELLA! THAT'S PROFESSOR VON VOLT'S ALARM!
WHOOP! WHOOP!
WHOOP! WHOOP!
PROFESSOR VON VOLT! HOW NICE TO HEAR FROM YOU! HOW ARE YOU? YES, OF COURSE. I'M COMING...
...RIGHT NOW!
IN AN INSTANT, I RUSHED TO PROFESSOR VON VOLT'S LAB. MY BEST FRIEND HAD SOME EXTRAORDINARY NEWS...
HERE I AM! I RACED OVER!
THANKS, GERONIMO! I HAVE TO SHOW YOU SOMETHING...
THIS NEW INSTRUMENT INDICATES ANY CHANGE THAT CROPS UP IN THE PAST.
THIS DISPLAY LETS ME KNOW WHEN THE PIRATE CATS ARE TRAVELING THROUGH TIME TO CHANGE HISTORY TO BENEFIT THEM... AND THAT'S EXACTLY WHAT'S HAPPENING NOW!
1492
THOSE PIRATE CATS! IT'S ALWAYS THEM! WHEN THEY TRAVEL TO THE PAST THEY ALSO CHANGE THE PRESENT. WE'VE GOT TO STOP THEM!
GERONIMO! YOU HAVE TO CALL YOUR FAMILY...
GULP! I REALLY THINK YOU'RE RIGHT!

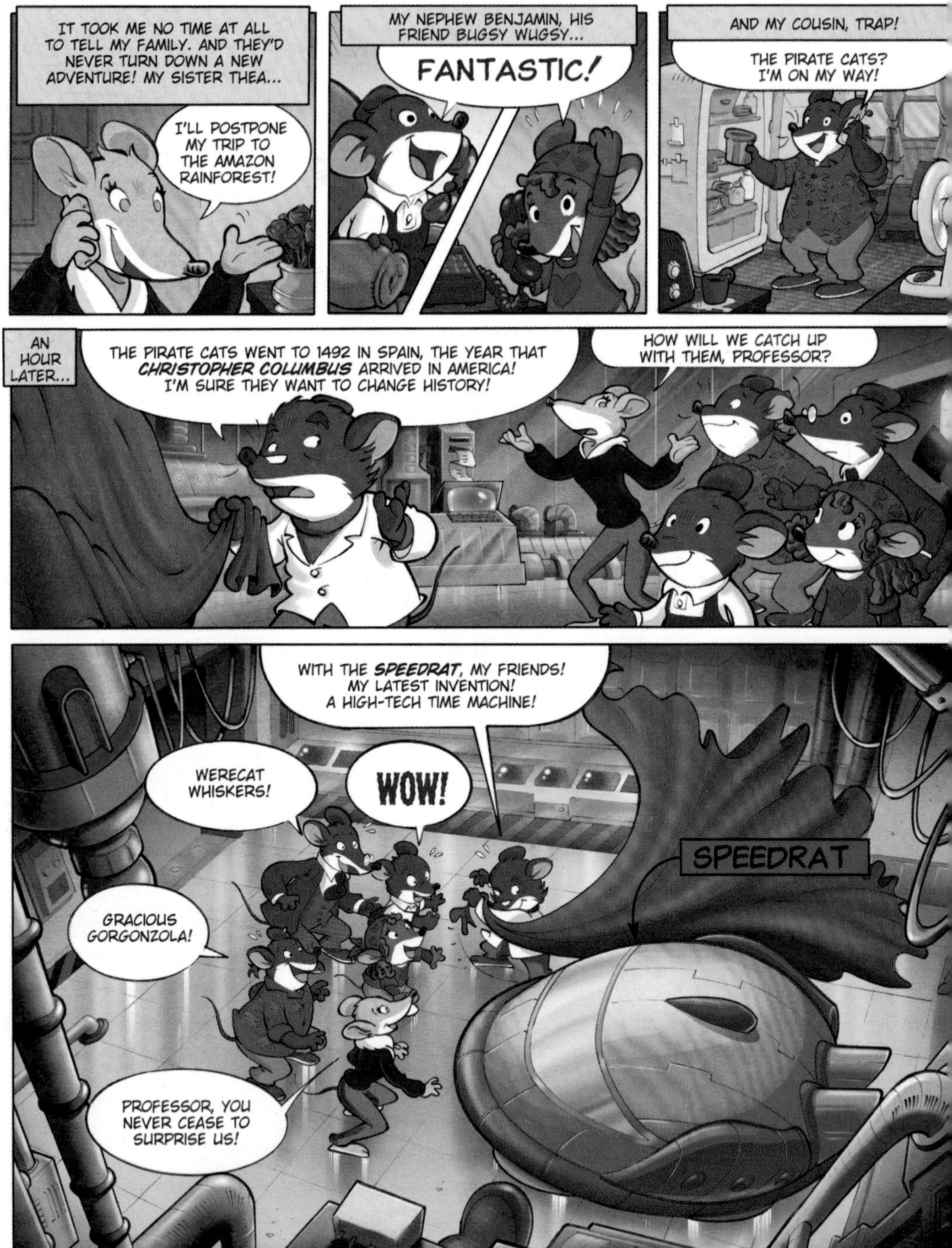
IT TOOK ME NO TIME AT ALL TO TELL MY FAMILY. AND THEY'D NEVER TURN DOWN A NEW ADVENTURE! MY SISTER THEA...
I'LL POSTPONE MY TRIP TO THE AMAZON RAINFOREST!
MY NEPHEW BENJAMIN, HIS FRIEND BUGSY WUGSY...
FANTASTIC!
AND MY COUSIN, TRAP!
THE PIRATE CATS? I'M ON MY WAY!
AN HOUR LATER...
THE PIRATE CATS WENT TO 1492 IN SPAIN, THE YEAR THAT CHRISTOPHER COLUMBUS ARRIVED IN AMERICA! I'M SURE THEY WANT TO CHANGE HISTORY!
HOW WILL WE CATCH UP WITH THEM, PROFESSOR?
WITH THE SPEEDRAT, MY FRIENDS! MY LATEST INVENTION! A HIGH-TECH TIME MACHINE!
WERECAT WHISKERS!
WOW!
SPEEDRAT
GRACIOUS GORGONZOLA!
PROFESSOR, YOU NEVER CEASE TO SURPRISE US!

HOW NICE! *ANOTHER TRIP IN TIME!* BUT...HOW WILL WE KEEP THEM FROM RECOGNIZING US?

YOU'LL FIND CLOTHING AND EVERYTHING YOU NEED FOR YOUR TRIP IN THE SPEEDRAT...

VRRRR

AND HOW WILL WE BE ABLE TO UNDERSTAND EVERYONE?

WITH THIS EARPIECE! IT'S PRACTICALLY INVISIBLE AND TRANSLATES EVERY LANGUAGE!

*GREAT!*

AND WHAT WILL WE EAT? MY STOMACH'S ALREADY *GROWLING--* ~ACK!~

UM, PROFESSOR, DON'T LISTEN TO HIM. TELL US WHERE THE PIRATE CATS ARE INSTEAD.

...GOOD LUCK! AND REMEMBER THAT THE *FUTURE IS IN YOUR PAWS!*

IN SPAIN, IN THE CITY OF PALOS, THE PORT THAT *COLUMBUS* SAILED FROM IN THE MONTH OF AUGUST...

NEVER FEAR, PROFESSOR! WE'LL FIND THE PIRATE CATS AND STOP THEM!

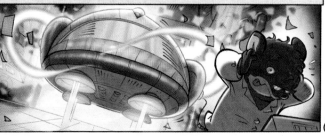

AND SO WE LEFT FOR A NEW TRIP INTO TIME! WE DIDN'T KNOW WHAT DANGERS WE WOULD FACE, BUT WE KNEW WE'D BE UP TO OUR WHISKERS IN ADVENTURE!

**PALOS** IS A SMALL TOWN TODAY, BUT IN THE TIME OF COLUMBUS IT WAS A LARGE PORT AND IT BECAME EVEN MORE IMPORTANT DUE TO THE DISCOVERY OF AMERICA!

Spain

Palos

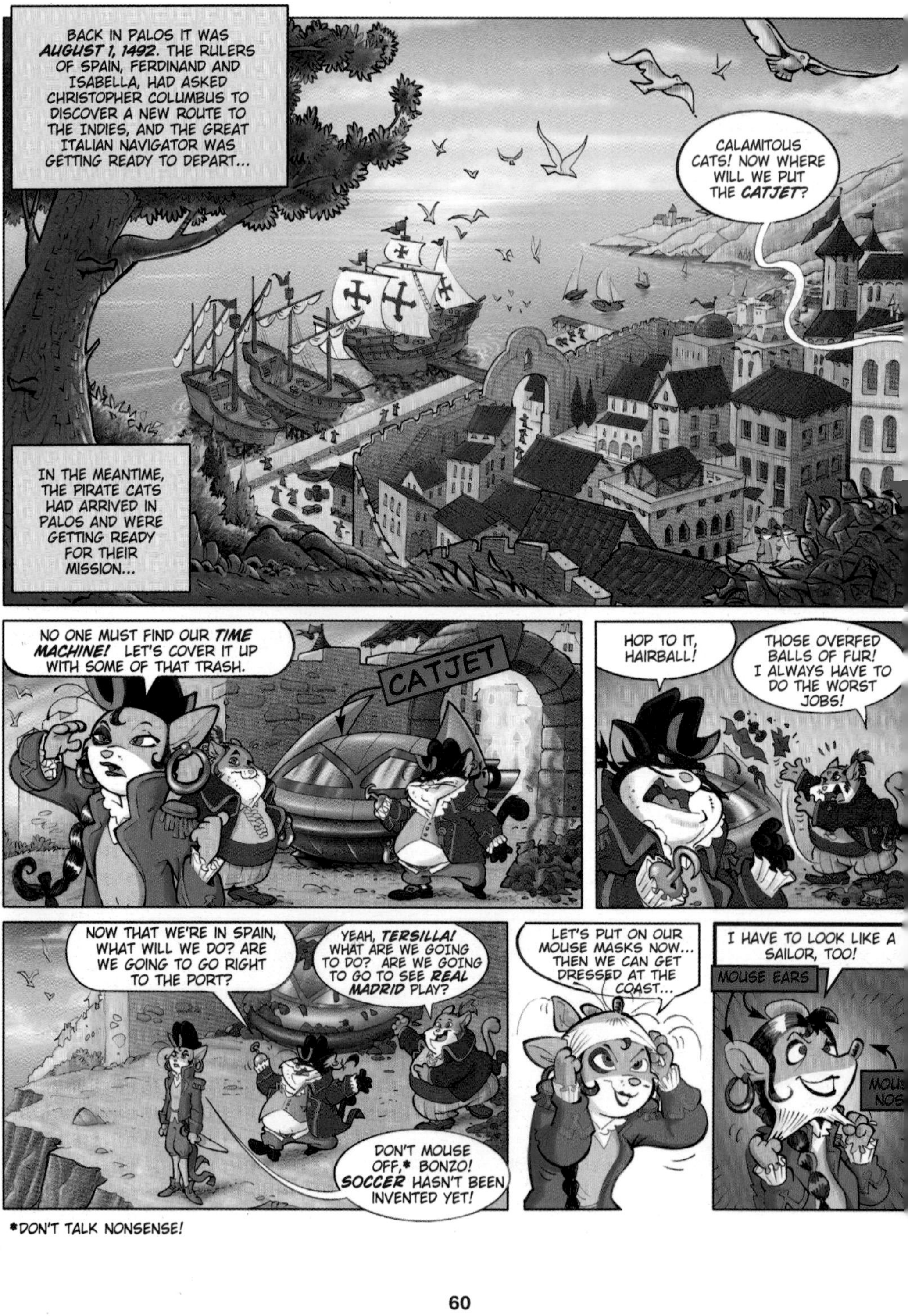
BACK IN PALOS IT WAS AUGUST 1, 1492. THE RULERS OF SPAIN, FERDINAND AND ISABELLA, HAD ASKED CHRISTOPHER COLUMBUS TO DISCOVER A NEW ROUTE TO THE INDIES, AND THE GREAT ITALIAN NAVIGATOR WAS GETTING READY TO DEPART...
CALAMITOUS CATS! NOW WHERE WILL WE PUT THE CATJET?
IN THE MEANTIME, THE PIRATE CATS HAD ARRIVED IN PALOS AND WERE GETTING READY FOR THEIR MISSION...
NO ONE MUST FIND OUR TIME MACHINE! LET'S COVER IT UP WITH SOME OF THAT TRASH.
CATJET
HOP TO IT, HAIRBALL!
THOSE OVERFED BALLS OF FUR! I ALWAYS HAVE TO DO THE WORST JOBS!
NOW THAT WE'RE IN SPAIN, WHAT WILL WE DO? ARE WE GOING TO GO RIGHT TO THE PORT?
YEAH, TERSILLA! WHAT ARE WE GOING TO DO? ARE WE GOING TO GO TO SEE REAL MADRID PLAY?
DON'T MOUSE OFF,* BONZO! SOCCER HASN'T BEEN INVENTED YET!
LET'S PUT ON OUR MOUSE MASKS NOW... THEN WE CAN GET DRESSED AT THE COAST...
I HAVE TO LOOK LIKE A SAILOR, TOO!
MOUSE EARS

*DON'T TALK NONSENSE!

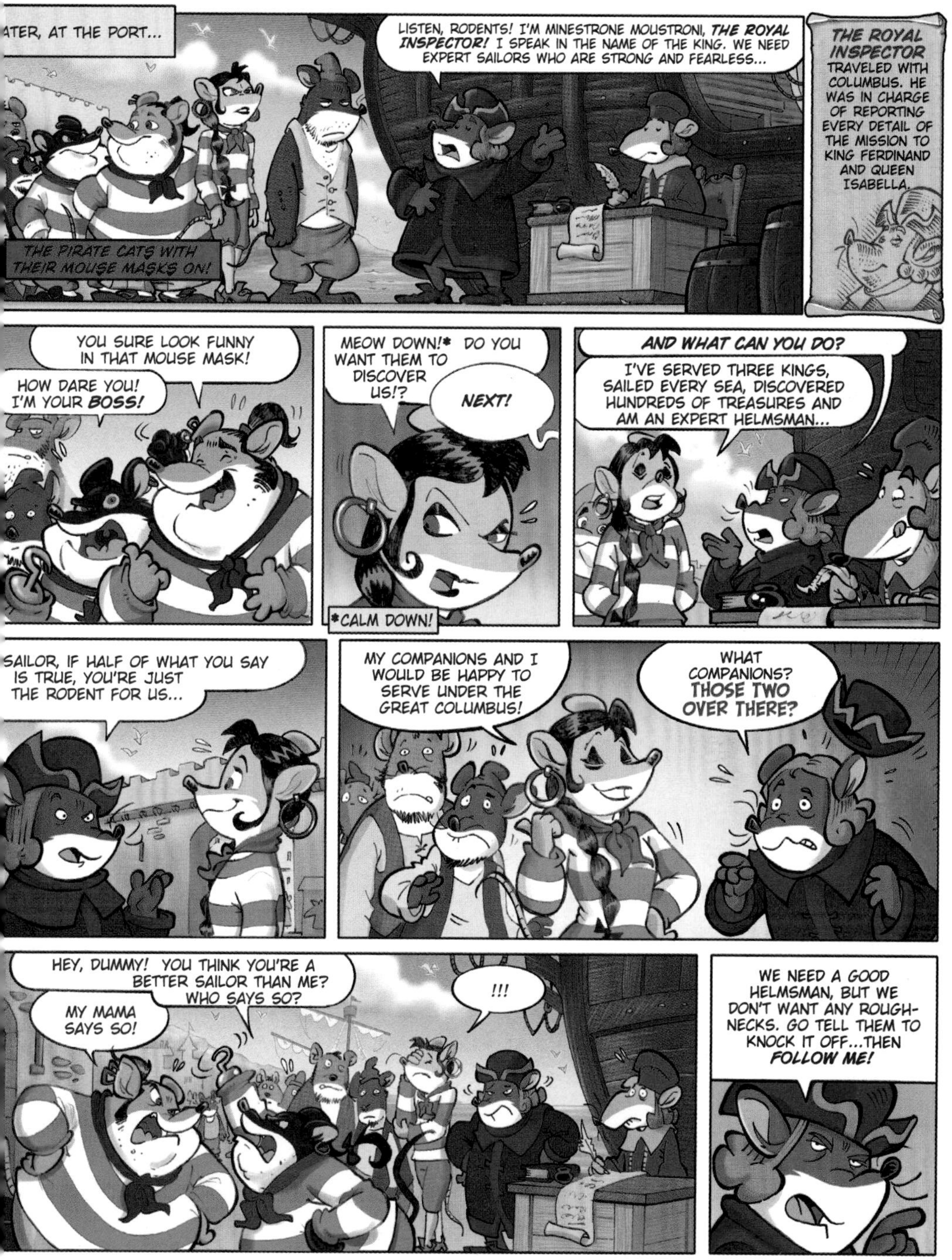
...LATER, AT THE PORT...
LISTEN, RODENTS! I'M MINESTRONE MOUSTRONI, THE ROYAL INSPECTOR! I SPEAK IN THE NAME OF THE KING. WE NEED EXPERT SAILORS WHO ARE STRONG AND FEARLESS...
THE ROYAL INSPECTOR TRAVELED WITH COLUMBUS. HE WAS IN CHARGE OF REPORTING EVERY DETAIL OF THE MISSION TO KING FERDINAND AND QUEEN ISABELLA.
THE PIRATE CATS WITH THEIR MOUSE MASKS ON!
YOU SURE LOOK FUNNY IN THAT MOUSE MASK!
HOW DARE YOU! I'M YOUR BOSS!
MEOW DOWN!* DO YOU WANT THEM TO DISCOVER US!?
NEXT!
*CALM DOWN!
AND WHAT CAN YOU DO?
I'VE SERVED THREE KINGS, SAILED EVERY SEA, DISCOVERED HUNDREDS OF TREASURES AND AM AN EXPERT HELMSMAN...
SAILOR, IF HALF OF WHAT YOU SAY IS TRUE, YOU'RE JUST THE RODENT FOR US...
MY COMPANIONS AND I WOULD BE HAPPY TO SERVE UNDER THE GREAT COLUMBUS!
WHAT COMPANIONS? THOSE TWO OVER THERE?
HEY, DUMMY! YOU THINK YOU'RE A BETTER SAILOR THAN ME? WHO SAYS SO?
MY MAMA SAYS SO!
!!!
WE NEED A GOOD HELMSMAN, BUT WE DON'T WANT ANY ROUGH-NECKS. GO TELL THEM TO KNOCK IT OFF...THEN FOLLOW ME!

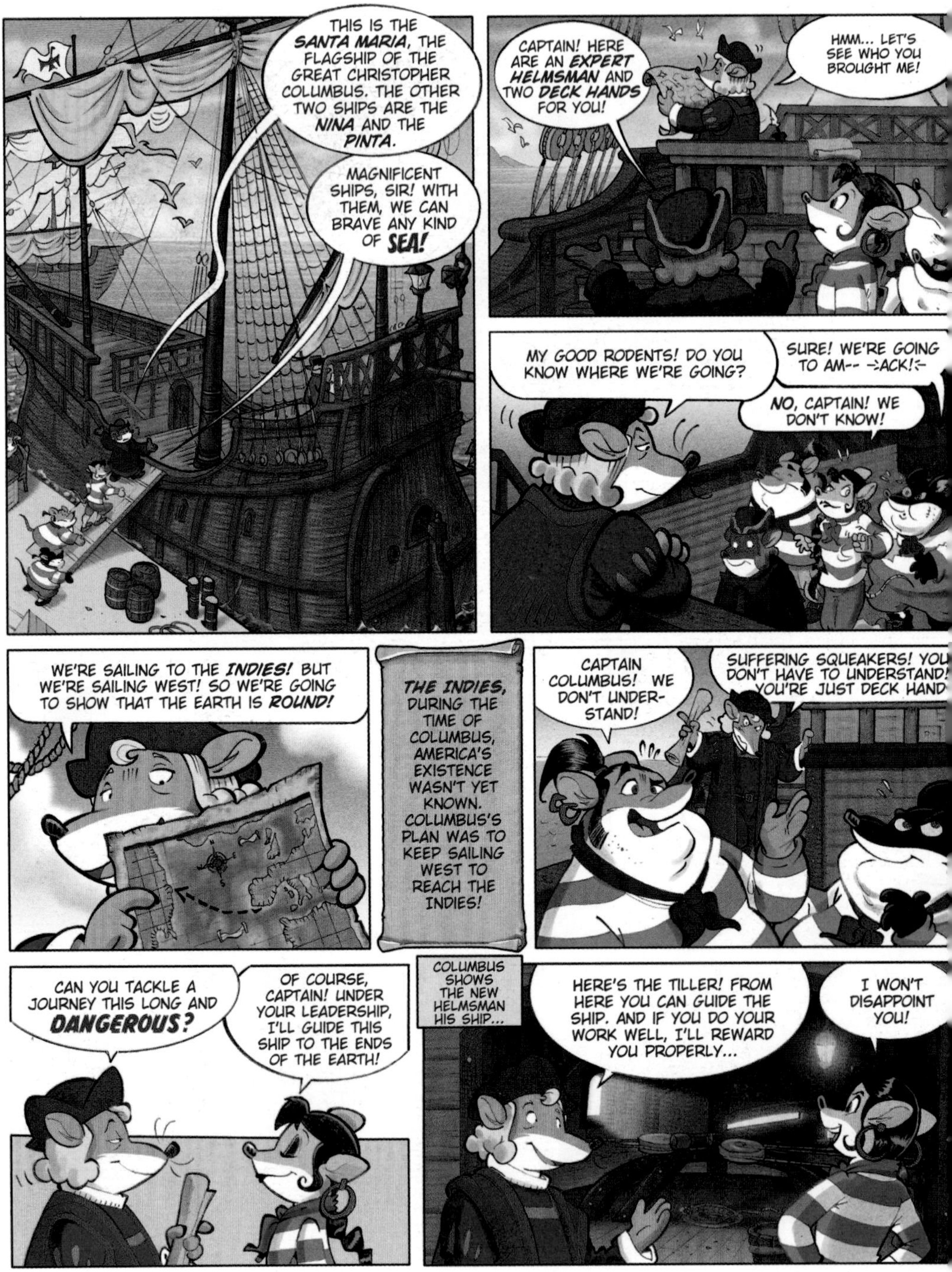
THIS IS THE SANTA MARIA, THE FLAGSHIP OF THE GREAT CHRISTOPHER COLUMBUS. THE OTHER TWO SHIPS ARE THE NINA AND THE PINTA.
MAGNIFICENT SHIPS, SIR! WITH THEM, WE CAN BRAVE ANY KIND OF SEA!
CAPTAIN! HERE ARE AN EXPERT HELMSMAN AND TWO DECK HANDS FOR YOU!
HMM... LET'S SEE WHO YOU BROUGHT ME!
MY GOOD RODENTS! DO YOU KNOW WHERE WE'RE GOING?
SURE! WE'RE GOING TO AM-- ACK!
NO, CAPTAIN! WE DON'T KNOW!
WE'RE SAILING TO THE INDIES! BUT WE'RE SAILING WEST! SO WE'RE GOING TO SHOW THAT THE EARTH IS ROUND!
THE INDIES, DURING THE TIME OF COLUMBUS, AMERICA'S EXISTENCE WASN'T YET KNOWN. COLUMBUS'S PLAN WAS TO KEEP SAILING WEST TO REACH THE INDIES!
CAPTAIN COLUMBUS! WE DON'T UNDER-STAND!
SUFFERING SQUEAKERS! YOU DON'T HAVE TO UNDERSTAND! YOU'RE JUST DECK HAND
CAN YOU TACKLE A JOURNEY THIS LONG AND DANGEROUS?
OF COURSE, CAPTAIN! UNDER YOUR LEADERSHIP, I'LL GUIDE THIS SHIP TO THE ENDS OF THE EARTH!
COLUMBUS SHOWS THE NEW HELMSMAN HIS SHIP...
HERE'S THE TILLER! FROM HERE YOU CAN GUIDE THE SHIP. AND IF YOU DO YOUR WORK WELL, I'LL REWARD YOU PROPERLY...
I WON'T DISAPPOINT YOU!

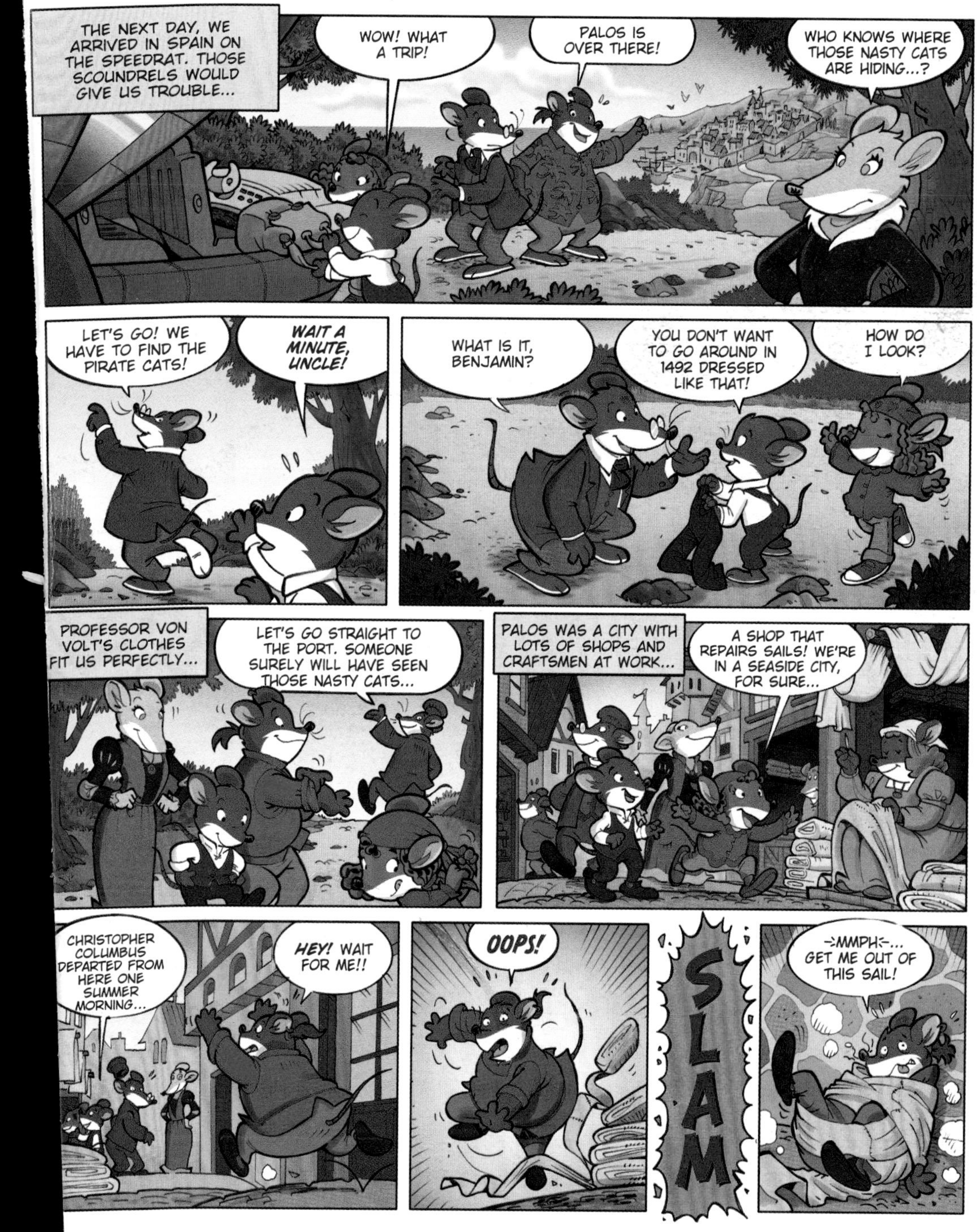

THE NEXT DAY, WE ARRIVED IN SPAIN ON THE SPEEDRAT. THOSE SCOUNDRELS WOULD GIVE US TROUBLE...
WOW! WHAT A TRIP!
PALOS IS OVER THERE!
WHO KNOWS WHERE THOSE NASTY CATS ARE HIDING...?
LET'S GO! WE HAVE TO FIND THE PIRATE CATS!
WAIT A MINUTE, UNCLE!
WHAT IS IT, BENJAMIN?
YOU DON'T WANT TO GO AROUND IN 1492 DRESSED LIKE THAT!
HOW DO I LOOK?
PROFESSOR VON VOLT'S CLOTHES FIT US PERFECTLY...
LET'S GO STRAIGHT TO THE PORT. SOMEONE SURELY WILL HAVE SEEN THOSE NASTY CATS...
PALOS WAS A CITY WITH LOTS OF SHOPS AND CRAFTSMEN AT WORK...
A SHOP THAT REPAIRS SAILS! WE'RE IN A SEASIDE CITY, FOR SURE...
CHRISTOPHER COLUMBUS DEPARTED FROM HERE ONE SUMMER MORNING...
HEY! WAIT FOR ME!!
OOPS!
SLAM
MMPH... GET ME OUT OF THIS SAIL!